WHY YOU'LL LOVE THIS BOOK
by Vivian French

Take one orphan (fun, feisty, and not in the least bit wimpy), add a wicked aunt (truly revolting and utterly vile) and a kind and enterprising nanny (full of brilliant ideas).

Mix them up with nuns, disguises and a mysterious traveller, and finally throw in Hilton Hall and millions of pounds. Result? A wonderful adventure story that's very VERY exciting!

Vivian French

Vivian French is the author of over two hundred children's books and several plays. She loves reading – especially books by Henrietta Branford.

Dimanche Diller

Diller

Henrietta Branford

Illustrated by
Rachel Merriman

HarperCollins *Children's Books*

First published in Great Britain by Collins in 1994
This edition published by HarperCollins *Children's Books* in 2010
HarperCollins *Children's Books* is a division of HarperCollins*Publishers* Ltd,
77-85 Fulham Palace Road, Hammersmith, London W6 8JB

The HarperCollins website address is
www.harpercollins.co.uk

1

ISBN-13 978-0-00-733396-7

Printed and bound in England by
Clays Ltd, St Ives plc

To Polly

One

Dimanche was three years old when Polly Pugh arrived at Hilton Hall, the house her parents had lived in before they were lost at sea when she was just a baby. And let me tell you right now, this is not one of those stories in which the missing parents turn up at the end. You must just take it from me that every now and then fate deals someone a cruel blow. It dealt Dimanche Diller several, and the first and the worst of them was the loss of her mother and father. This is how it happened.

Sailing in their yacht *Hippolytus* among the rocky islands of the Cyclades, the Dillers were set upon by one of those storms that seem to come from nowhere. In a matter of seconds the sea had turned from blue to purple, and billows of black cloud had blotted out the summer sky.

"Cut loose sheets, Dolores! We're carrying too much sail," Darcy shouted above the sound of creaking wood and snapping canvas. "Batten down the hatches! You and Dimanche man the lifeboat."

Dimanche's mother was nothing if not thorough, and it was her thoroughness, even in the face of mortal danger, that saved her baby daughter's life. She bundled Dimanche into her tiny lifejacket, wrapped her in a blanket and tied her securely to the thwart. She kissed her, and turned towards her husband.

"Don't wait for me," he shouted. "I must belay the mizzen! You get in with Dimanche."

At that very moment, a monster of a wave, as strong as steel, rose high above the little boat, hung for a moment like a cliff of glass, and crashed on to the deck. It cracked the boat from stem to stern, splintered the mast, ripped through the sails, and tore baby Dimanche from her mother's arms, casting the lifeboat and its precious cargo adrift upon the sea.

Dimanche cried and struggled as the storm drove her fragile boat far to the south and west. All night the great waves surged, tossing the lifeboat like a cork. Salt sea spray soaked Dimanche's blanket, and an east wind turned her tiny face and hands to ice.

At dawn the next day, a fisherman from Kithira saw what he thought must be an empty lifeboat, rising and falling on the steady swell. He pulled in his net, and rowed across to take a look, hauling the battered lifeboat alongside with a boathook. Imagine his surprise when, looking in, he saw Dimanche, lying in a tangle of blanket in the bottom!

"Aphrodite, Goddess of Love and Beauty," he whispered, "who floated in her scallop shell past this very island, was not more beautiful than this child." Tearing off his jumper, he wrapped the baby in it and rowed for home, marvelling as he did so at the birthmark on the baby's wrist: it was just the shape of his own island of Kithira.

He and his wife were sorely tempted to keep the child, and how different this story would have been if they had done so. But they were parents themselves, and they could imagine all too well the frightful misery of this child's mother and father, if they were still alive.

Sadly they gave her to the village priest, whose job it was to care for foundlings.

The priest took Dimanche by plane to Athens, on the mainland, and handed her over to the police. By this time the wreckage of the *Hippolytus* had been discovered, washed up on the coast of Milos. Helicopters were searching every square mile of sea from Samos down to Crete and northwards to the Sporades but neither Darcy nor Dolores was ever found.

The Greek police handed Dimanche over to someone from the Red Cross, who flew her back to London and placed her in the loving care of the Sisters of Small Mercies. In due course the following advertisement appeared in the personal column of *The Times*:

FOUND DRIFTING IN THE MEDITERRANEAN SEA, it said, **DIMANCHE DILLER, BABY DAUGHTER OF DARCY AND DOLORES DILLER, BOTH BELIEVED LOST AT SEA.**

There was a number to ring and an address to write to.

If you are wondering how the nuns knew Dimanche's name, it was because her mother Dolores was so very thorough.

She had sewn tiny embroidered name tapes into every one of Dimanche's clothes: her babygrow, her vest, her nappy, even her plastic pants, all bore her name in letters of pink silk. How did they know that Darcy and Dolores were the names of her late parents? The Greek Rescue Service had found the lost yacht's log book, sealed in polythene and washed ashore with the wreckage. It gave them details of her course, and the names of the three people who had sailed in her. So far as anybody knew, it was all that remained to Dimanche of her dear parents.

Two

I'm sorry to tell you that there were hundreds of bogus replies to the advertisement. It occurred to many people that an orphaned baby, sole survivor from the wreck of a luxury yacht, might well be worth a fortune, even though she was just a tiny, helpless baby, unable so much as to wipe her own nose – or anything else, for that matter. The nuns sensibly decided to ask the police for help, and Chief Superintendent Barry Bullpit took on the case. He went over each and every person who claimed to be a relation of Dimanche's most carefully, and rejected all of them.

For a while, no further candidates came forward. The nuns made a great fuss of baby Dimanche, and she had as nice a time as any orphan can. Mother Superior carried her up and down whenever she cried. Sister Sophia and Sister Catriona made her a little hammock to remind her of her seafaring days with her dear parents, and slung it between two lilac trees in the convent garden. There they would rock her gently, singing songs and sea shanties and even, I'm sorry to say, arguing with one another over who should be allowed to change her nappy.

Three

It was almost one year later that a large, bad-tempered person whose name was Valburga Vilemile noticed the advertisement in an old copy of *The Times*, which she was using to line her cat's earth tray.

Most cats are clean and independent animals. Not Cyclops. He was a cowardly bully, too lazy to go outside to do his business. He insisted on a smelly earth tray in the kitchen, and he would not attempt to defend his territory in the garden and chase out other tom cats –

the only cats he'd fight with were not cats but kittens. He had a matted coat the colour of mud and his tail was thin and stringy because he never washed at all. His legs bent outwards at the elbows under the weight of his body and he had, as you'll have guessed, only one eye. For all that, his mistress loved him, which only goes to show that there's a trace of good in even the meanest person.

Valburga paused in her revolting task, adjusted her hat, and scanned the Personal Column. **FOUND ADRIFT…** she read. **DIMANCHE… BELOVED DAUGHTER OF DARCY AND DOLORES…** She read the whole advertisement. She read it several times, and stopped to scratch under her hat. All her life she had thought a great deal about money and how to get it. It did not take her long to come up with a plan.

"If we play our cards right, Cyclops," she said, "this could mean champagne for me and caviar for you. Pickled sturgeon-roe, Cyclops. How about that?"

Valburga went at once to her local library and looked in a large book called *Who's Who*. It lists all sorts of rich and famous people, and says where they live and what they like to have for breakfast, how many children they have and what their favourite pastimes are. She soon found Darcy and Dolores Diller, and was pleased to find that their ancestral home was Hilton Hall, a handsome mansion overlooking the little village of Hilton in the Hollow. By lucky chance this was the very place where her old schoolfriend Gussie now held the job of post mistress and village shopkeeper. Gussie and Valburga had been pupils at Coldcrust Court Approved School for Girls. They shared happy memories of midnight feasts, impromptu bonfires, and other diversions. Valburga felt sure that Gussie would help her with her plan.

She disguised herself with a wig and a pair of dark glasses, and went straight to Hilton Hall. There, posing as a double glazing salesperson, she made young Cosmo the gardener show her round the whole house. While pretending to measure the huge old windows in the drawing room, she was able to take a quick look in Darcy Diller's desk. She removed a photograph and a letter, both of which she felt sure would come in useful.

She also spent a morning in the local church, looking at plaques and gravestones. She told the vicar that she was writing a book about the historic village of Hilton in the Hollow. She asked him to tell her all about everyone who lived there, but he soon smelt a rat and sent her packing. So she went along to the Post Office, and spent a happy evening chewing over old times with Gussie, and listening to all the gossip of the village.

By the end of three days she knew all about Hilton in the Hollow, and everyone who lived there. "Now for my habit," she said to Gussie. This needed a visit to a theatrical costume maker, and Valburga found one in a nearby town without much difficulty.

Just seven days later this neatly written letter arrived on Chief Superintendent Barry Bullpit's desk:

Cher Monsieur,

I am the last remaining relative of the child Dimanche Diller. I have been living in a convent in France for some years, following a tragic personal loss. It is for this reason that I have only just happened upon the advertisement announcing the death of my dear sister Dolores and her husband Darcy, and the lone survival of their daughter, my niece, dearest Dimanche.

I long to be reunited with her. Please arrange it as soon as possible.

Your sincerely,

Sister Verity Victorine.

P.S. I enclose a photo taken of myself with my sister Dolores shortly before my departure for France. Of course I have not met my little niece. She was not yet born by the time I left this country. However, I feel I know her intimately from my dear sister's letters – even down to the dear little birthmark on her wrist, that is shaped like the island of Kithira.

The letter was sealed with a blob of red sealing wax in which were stamped the letters VV.

The Chief Superintendent read the letter carefully, and studied the faded old photograph. He scratched his chin, and studied them again. He sent them across to the forensic laboratories for testing. He ran them through the police computer backwards, forwards and sideways. He gave them to sniffer dogs to sniff, and to experts to analyse. He took them home and showed them to his wife. In the end he decided that they were genuine. Even the best policemen make mistakes, as you will see by reading any newspaper.

Barry Bullpit invited the writer of the letter to meet him at the convent of the Sisters of Small Mercies, having first checked with Mother Superior as to when would be a convenient time.

"No time," poor Mother Superior whispered in her

heart of hearts. "No time would be convenient for you to take Dimanche from us." But, just like the fisherman's wife in far-off Kithira, who still thought often and longingly of the baby from the sea, she knew it was her duty to return Dimanche to the bosom of what family she had left. "Come to tea on Tuesday," she said graciously. "Bring Sister Victorine. Every orphan deserves a long-lost aunt." Mothers Superior also make mistakes.

It was not a happy meeting. The nuns gathered sadly in their sunny parlour. Honey from their own bees, bread baked in their own ovens, fruit teas made from rosehips and camomile picked from the convent garden, and golden butter churned by the sisters' careful hands lay like treasure on the linen cloth. Sun streamed in through the stone-arched windows and lit on little Dimanche, sitting in her high chair and banging on her tray with a silver spoon. Sister Sophia sat on one side of her and fed her titbits of bread and honey dipped in milk. Sister Catriona sat on the other and dabbed at the little girl's chin and fingers with a soft napkin. It was a sight to bring joy to any heart, but the hearts of the Sisters of Small Mercies were filled with sorrow.

Mother Superior sat at the head of the table, with

the chief superintendent on her left and Dimanche's long-lost aunt on her right. The Sisters of Small Mercies were quite surprised by the aunt's appearance, perhaps because she was one of those people who seem to be bigger than their clothes. She was not fat in that nice, billowy way some people are, so that when you lean against them you feel comfortable. No. She was fat in a bossy, get-out-of-my-way-or-I'll-squash-you-flat sort of way. Her face, what they could see of it behind her veil, was reddish. Not a nice reddish-brown, like someone who's been outdoors a lot, but an I'm-so-angry-I-may-explode-at-any-minute sort of red. She wore a signet ring on her little finger with her initials on it: VV. Her heavy veil made eating and drinking quite difficult for her and she spilled cake crumbs down the front of her navy blue habit. She got her tea cup mixed up with her rosary, and she forgot to wait for grace. She seemed to the Sisters to be a peculiar sort of nun, and not a very nice one. They supposed that her strange ways had something to do with her having lived abroad. French nuns are quite different from us, they thought. None of them had ever been to France.

Dimanche was placed at the far end of the table from her visitors, because she was inclined to throw things.

The nuns didn't mind a bit, but they felt it better that such important visitors should be seated out of range. The strange Sister didn't in any case seem anxious to get close to her niece. When Sister Sophia held her out to be kissed, she backed away as if she had been asked to kiss a spider.

"It is a great sacrifice to one of my powerful vocation," she told them, "to leave my dear convent and all my dear Sisters in France. But my Mother Superior says that I must do my familial duty, and I am accustomed to obeying her in all things."

Dimanche stared doubtfully up from Sister Sophia's lap at her new-found relation, and dribbled.

"Oh, the darling," murmured Sister Catriona, dabbing at her chin with a bib. "Isn't she enchanting?"

Dimanche's new aunt did not look enchanted, in fact she looked revolted, but she did her best to disguise her feelings. The veil helped. If they had been able to see through the veil, the Sisters of Small Mercies would have found her face most unpleasant.

"Time to go," the strange Sister announced, as soon as tea was finished.

"Already?" faltered Mother Superior. She wiped her eyes and frowned at Sisters Sophia and Catriona, who were beginning to sob. "Please understand, Sister Victorine, that here at the Convent of Small Mercies, we have grown to love Dimanche very much. We are glad, of course, as we ought to be, that you have come to claim her. It's a wonderful thing to have your family around you, and we wish you every joy with little Dimanche. But we cannot help crying, now that it's time for her to go."

"There is no need for you to give her another thought," said the strange nun crossly. "I shall engage someone suitable to care for her until she's old enough to go to boarding school. I shall choose one in the north of England, one with plenty of discipline and outdoor activities. How lucky she is that I noticed your advertisement! Now, put her in the pram, ladies, I mean Sisters, and we'll be off."

"Where are you taking her, Sister Victorine?" asked Mother Superior. "If it's not too far away, we would so love to visit her."

"That will not be possible. I'm taking her to our ancestral home at Hilton in the Hollow. It is a remote spot, and inhospitable."

"But you will write to us, Sister Victorine?"

"Probably not. I shall have my devotions to attend to, as well as my niece."

There was not a dry eye in the convent as Dimanche

was tucked into the big black pram that the nuns had bought for her, and wheeled away towards the station. Even Chief Superintendent Barry Bullpit had to wipe away his tears. He was not an emotional man, but when he was telling his wife about it that evening, he found himself crying all over again.

"I can't explain it, Beryl," he said. "Seeing that scrap of an orphan lying there as good as gold, and that old dragon of a Sister pushing her away down the road in a big black pram, and the poor nuns crying fit to burst, it got to me."

Beryl Bullpit made her husband a cup of hot chocolate and sat him down in front of the TV.

"You watch the sport, Barry," she advised. "And don't upset yourself. Your job is not an easy one."

As for the nuns, their last glimpse of their precious foundling had to last them for many a long year. It was a good thing that they were able to find solace in prayer, otherwise I'm sure their hearts would have been broken.

Four

The journey should have been a dismal one for little Dimanche.

Her new aunt left her alone in her pram in the luggage compartment, with a bottle of cold tea propped beside her pillow, and went off by herself for cakes and ale in the restaurant car.

If it had not been for a kind-hearted guard called Winston, who knows how Dimanche would have managed? Fortunately, Winston was a father and a grandfather, and what he didn't know about babies wouldn't fill a thimble. He fetched warm milk, and banana sandwiches, and made Dimanche's journey pleasant by singing to her.

Valburga Vilemile did not show up until the train pulled into Hilton in the Hollow station. Winston felt extremely angry with her as he helped her down with the pram.

"Look here, Sister," he said. "You may be a nun but you don't know a thing about babies. Babies need plenty of attention. They need food and drink all the time. They need conversation. They need looking at, picking up, and singing to. They need cheerful and abundant company by day and by night. Why d'you think their parents look so tired?"

"I suggest, my good man, that you confine your attention to the serving of tea and coffee, the lifting down of prams, and the occasional clipping of tickets," Valburga replied. "Unless you wish to be reported to your superiors for insolence."

Winston shook his head and clicked his fingers. He peeped into the pram. "Good luck, little one," he murmured. "You're going to need it."

How right he was.

Five

Dimanche's new life, without her parents, or the nuns, and with her peculiar new aunt, was not an easy one. Dozens of nannies passed through Hilton Hall, and some were delightful and some were frightful but all of them gave in their notice within a month or two.

Those who liked babies at all loved Dimanche. They couldn't help it. She was adorable. By the time she was two, she was running up and down the long gloomy corridors of the big old house, opening doors, turning out cupboards, posting things down the lavatory, investigating dustbins, and doing all the things an enterprising baby should do. Her curly dark hair shone like hens' feathers, and her round, brown eyes peered out from behind her fringe in a way that made you think of a hedgehog under a bush. Her little fat feet went pitter patter on the stone-flagged floors, leaving behind them a delicate tracery of tiny footprints marked out in whatever it was she had most recently been playing in – mud, if she'd been in the flower beds; sand, if the sandpit; talcum powder, if the bath. It drove her aunt wild. "Clean this mess up!" she'd shout at the unfortunate nanny. "Do it now and do it properly! Lock the child into her room and don't let her out!"

The better ones would kiss Dimanche goodbye and head for the station at this point. Nobody nice would agree to shutting a two-year-old into her bedroom, after all. The nastier ones would linger on a while, and during these times Dimanche would have been truly unhappy if it hadn't been for Cosmo the gardener. He would tiptoe up the back stairs with a punnet of strawberries or a bowl of redcurrants in his hands, or a bunch of crunchy carrots, or a tomato warm from the sun. "Look what I've got for you, Dimanche," he'd say. He'd shoo Cyclops away – he couldn't abide cats because of the way they caught nestlings in the spring, and dug up his flower beds. Then he'd sit down beside Dimanche and feed her titbits, and tell her stories, and show her interesting things from out-of-doors.

He brought her a last year's blackbird's nest, all scratchy and rough on the outside, but lined with mud as smooth as satin on the inside. He brought her hairy caterpillars to look at, and snail shells to add to her collection, and sometimes a frog in his hat. If he brought something alive, they would watch it together for a while before returning it carefully to that part of the garden where Cosmo had found it.

Whenever Dimanche was feeling sad, she would go outdoors and look for Cosmo. If he was busy, she'd help him with his work. If not, they'd play together, or sit in the greenhouse while he told her riddles and jokes and played cat's cradle with green garden string. Cosmo had six twiddly fingers on each hand, instead of five, and this made him particularly good at cat's cradle.

"Is that old aunt of yours making you miserable?"

he'd ask. "Don't let her! Come and talk to me while I weed the spinach, and I'll tell you stories from when your gran was little."

"Can you remember when my gran was little?" Dimanche asked.

Cosmo shook his head. "No. But I'm a friend of Old Tom Shovel the gravedigger, and he knows everything about everything. Especially if your family comes into it. I can't make out how that aunt of yours comes to be part of your family at all. She's nothing like the rest of them, from what Tom Shovel says. Funny thing is, she reminds me of somebody. Can't think who. Here, try one of these plums, they're ripe as rain."

Whenever the aunt caught Cosmo talking to Dimanche, she'd dock a day's pay from his wages, and send Dimanche off to bed, but both of them felt it was worth the risk.

One of the nicest of the nannies got the sack for letting Dimanche make mud pies on the grand stone steps in front of Hilton Hall. Valburga was on her way to the village to buy Cyclops a few treats – pigs' ears, sheep's eyes, that sort of thing. She didn't look where she was putting her feet.

"What is the meaning of this filthy mess?" she roared.

"It's mud pies, Madam," the nanny answered. "Children make them. They need to. It helps them to develop, psychologically."

"Psychological nothing!" Madam roared. "I don't pay you to develop her psychologically! I pay you to keep her out of my way! You're fired!"

When she got back from the village she rang London and ordered another nanny. "And send someone suitable this time!" she shouted. "I want someone from a military background. I've had enough of namby-pamby nannies with soft ideas about warm milk and nursery rhymes. What this child needs is discipline!"

"We do have one young lady from a military background, Madam," faltered the lady from the nanny agency. "But Lady Cruddle has reserved her. We've got an excellent person from the prison service, but Sir Brigham Brogue wants her for his difficult daughter. In fact, the demand for nannies has quite outstripped the supply for the time being. You yourself have already run through a dozen or so of our best candidates, Madam. To tell the truth I've only got one left, and I doubt if she would suit. Her name is Polly Pugh."

"Send her down."

That was how Polly Pugh arrived at Hilton Hall. It just happened that she arrived on Dimanche's third birthday. Not that she would have known this. Dimanche did not know herself, and the aunt would certainly not have mentioned it – but the Sisters of Small Mercies had sent Dimanche, by train, a cherry cake with white icing and three candles, so Polly Pugh guessed. Around the outside of the cake was a circle of little dancing nuns made of fondant icing. In the centre there were golden marzipan beehives, and out of them flew a cloud of tiny bees that spelt out HAPPY BIRTHDAY, DEAREST DIMANCHE.

"How gorgeous! How scrumptious! How beautiful!" cried Polly Pugh. "What time's the party?"

"Party, Miss Pugh? There'll be no party."

"Why ever not, Madam?"

"My niece doesn't deserve one. She's never had one and she's not starting now."

Polly Pugh was deeply shocked. She had always thought of nuns as kind-hearted people. She decided then and there that she was going to get the better of this one, no matter how hard it was, no matter how long it took. She made herself a promise, and she kept it.

Dimanche could tell just by looking at Polly Pugh that they were going to like each other. Polly was tall and thin with long arms and legs and a very nice springy way of walking. Her eyes were light blue, large, shining, and beautifully shaped with soft shadowy eyelids, and dark coloured eyelashes that had a little curl at the ends. Her hair was that shade of red that makes you think of silk scarves and traffic lights. She liked to wear pretty clothes on some days and old jeans on others, but whatever she wore, she looked terrific. *Like a queen*, Dimanche thought. She behaved like one too, if queens are brave and loyal, which is what they're supposed to be.

Polly Pugh was not afraid of her employer. She knew, because the agency had told her, that they were never going to send another nanny to Hilton Hall, and she let her employer know this – not in so many words, of course, that would not have been polite – but she made it clear that if she, Polly Pugh, was sacked, that would be it. Finito. All in all, Polly Pugh felt certain that she would not be sacked. She felt even more certain that Dimanche Diller was the child for her.

Six

Polly Pugh's employer encouraged her to take Dimanche away on holiday every summer – provided, of course, that Polly paid for everything out of her wages. Since Polly's wages were extremely small – all nannies' wages are, I don't know why – these holidays were not luxurious. That couldn't have mattered less. In fact, it was probably more fun that way.

Polly bought a little tent, just big enough for two, and a little stove, and two saucepans, and two mugs and two plates and two knives and two forks. She also bought two sleeping bags and two pairs of gumboots and two mackintoshes, all of which you have to have for camping. For several summers, she and Dimanche spent the month of August under canvas.

At first these holidays were taken by the seaside. Long summer days were spent staring into rock pools, building strange and complicated sand structures, paddling, and later swimming in the small green waves, or just sunbathing. In the evenings Polly and Dimanche cooked delicious meals, sang, and played duets on their harmonicas.

Polly was surprised, as time went on, to find that her employer suggested increasingly daring holidays. Polly knew that children need adventure, but she had not expected her employer to feel the same. In the past she had shown absolutely no understanding of what a growing child needs.

"Teach the child deep-sea diving," she suggested, as soon as Dimanche could swim. "Never mind the treacherous tides, you mustn't mollycoddle her. At her age I could swim the channel with my eyes shut." This was completely untrue – Valburga couldn't swim a stroke and never had been able to. "Take her somewhere warm and tropical, Miss Pugh. Somewhere with large and interesting fish." Luckily this particular idea came to nothing, because of how much money it costs to go somewhere warm and tropical.

As Dimanche grew older, she developed a keen interest in rock climbing. This is often done in cold, wet places, and need not cost much money, once you've got the right equipment. Polly and Dimanche could not have afforded to buy theirs, so the vicar of Hilton in the Hollow helped them out. He was a doughty climber, and a generous man, and he lent them everything they needed. Polly felt sure that it was safe to borrow ropes and things from him because he kept his climbing gear in excellent condition.

He came with them on their first few expeditions, and gave them useful and interesting lessons in map reading, compass work, abseiling and belaying. Together they visited some of the wildest parts of England, Scotland and Wales in search of testing climbs.

Valburga was all for it. "Have fun!" she'd bellow – which was not a bit like her. She took out library books and familiarised herself with all the most difficult routes. "Why not try the Devil's Drop?" she suggested, on their second outing. "It's perfect for beginners.

Or what about the Transylvanian Traverse?" She seemed to be egging them on.

Polly and Dimanche ignored all her suggestions and listened instead to the vicar's advice, and their own good sense. Even so, they had one near-disaster. It happened on their first visit to the island of Skye.

They pitched their tent in a boulder field and began to scramble up the gently angled slabs of smooth dark rock. They climbed steadily upwards until they reached their first obstacle – a bulging forehead of rock which leaned out in an overhanging curve. Polly was leading, carefully choosing her belaying points as she climbed. Dimanche followed. Below their feet a lark sang, and off in the distance shafts of light came and went over the Cuillin Sound. At the very limit of their gaze lay the magical islands of Rhum and Eigg.

Towards the top of the overhang, Polly began to feel that something was wrong. Things can change quite dramatically from one second to the next when you are climbing, and Polly knew that a good climber listens to the secret messages we call intuition.

She began to examine the spike of rock round which she'd wound her main rope. The rock was good. Solid, dark and strong. No danger there. She ran her hand along the rope. Almost at once her thumb encountered a deep nick in the fibre – not a tear worn by the rocks of Sky, but the clean, sharp work of a knife. A less courageous person might have lost her nerve at this point. Polly didn't.

"My rope's damaged, Dimanche," she called down calmly. "I'm going to use my slings and karabiners to get down to you. Don't be afraid. Wait where you are. When I reach you we'll use your rope and abseil down."

Dimanche clung to the rock face patiently. She breathed steadily, careful not to let fear spoil her concentration. Below her the cliff curved in and away, leaving an empty gulf beneath her feet.

When at last Polly got down to Dimanche, using every little knot and knobble of rock that she could find, she was beginning to shake a little. Dimanche chose a safe belaying point and together she and Polly made a careful descent.

Neither of them ever knew for certain how the rope came to be cut. It had been in immaculate condition when the vicar gave it to them. But cut it was, in half a dozen places. Polly had her suspicions, but she kept them to herself. From then on she checked and checked again every inch of rope, every piton, every karabiner that she and Dimanche used.

One of the best holidays they went on, it must have been the year Dimanche was nine, was pony trekking. It took a large part of Polly's wages, and all of Dimanche's pocket money for many months, and even so they almost didn't save enough. In the end, one of Dimanche's brainwaves saved the day.

Off in the woods – there were woods and fields all round Hilton Hall, as well as a trout stream, and even a lake with islands in the middle – off in the woods, some distance from the big house, families of travelling people were in the habit of stopping to pick primroses, suck eggs, and do the clever country things those people sometimes do. Luckily the aunt did not know about this, or she would have had them all evicted.

In addition to whittling clothes pegs and making wax flowers for sale from door to door, the families traded in scrap metal. Travelling people were among the first to appreciate the importance of recycling things. It is a traditional occupation with them, and one of the things these families recycled was old cars. The cars were often rusty and muddy, but some of them were still too good for scrap and these needed a thorough wash and polish. In return for a small sum, Dimanche would wash and polish an averagely dirty car. If it was really filthy, she would charge a little more, and the travellers were happy to pay her. Their own children, like children everywhere, refused to wash cars for their parents. They would wash them for neighbours, for money, or not at all. These children had no neighbours, apart from rabbits and squirrels and pheasants and so on, and these have neither cars nor money.

Whenever Dimanche could slip away from Hilton Hall without her aunt noticing, she did. She'd call in at the greenhouse where Cosmo hid her bucket and sponge, and her polishes and dusters, and off she'd go. She earned nearly thirty pounds in just three weeks. It was enough to tip the balance. The pony trekking holiday was on.

They went in August, because the aunt was taking a cruise to the Bahamas then, and she didn't want Dimanche hanging round the house and getting up to mischief while she was away. They took their tent, and though they had not got the proper riding clothes, they soon found this didn't matter a bit. Climbing requires precisely the right equipment. For riding, all you need is a hard hat and a pony.

The holiday was to take place in the New Forest, somewhere neither Polly nor Dimanche had ever visited. Polly bought a map before they went so that they could familiarise themselves with the terrain, and they found a great many strange names on it. Strodgemoor Bottom and Mockbeggar in the north, Hag Hill, Pig Bush and Woodfidley in the south, as well as Tiptoe and Sway, which sounded to Dimanche more like dances than places. The rivers and streams had interesting names as well – Dimanche particularly liked the sound of Worts Gutter. There was also a dear little winding stream called Dockens Water that she hoped to explore.

It was on the day they searched for the source of the Dockens Water that the accident happened. Dimanche's pony was a handsome New Forest animal, dark bay in colour, that's to say dark brown with a black mane and tail. He was gentle without being dull. His large eyes noticed everything, and he often seemed to spot things Dimanche couldn't see. His name was Hightown Trotter.

The trek wasn't one of those where you have to keep in line, and Trotter had wandered away from the other ponies. He had noticed a particularly sweet-looking tuft of heather growing by the side of the road. He stopped, and Dimanche had loosened her reins to let him take a mouthful, when suddenly she felt him grow tense. He lifted his head and listened.

Then two things happened, both rather suddenly. A long black limousine shot round the corner and surged across the road, and Trotter leapt at the hedge, cleared it, and landed, snorting, on the far side. Dimanche took off with Trotter but landed several feet further on in a patch of bracken.

Polly Pugh cantered over to where Dimanche sat and slid off her pony's back. "Are you hurt, Dimanche?" she asked. "Is anything broken?"

"No, I'm fine, Polly. So's Trotter. Did you see the way he jumped out of the way of that car?"

"But where did it come from?" Polly asked. "It must have been doing eighty miles an hour! Did you get a look at the driver, Dimanche?"

"No, I was too busy falling off to see a thing. Did you?"

"Not really."

This wasn't strictly true. Polly had seen enough to notice that the driver looked familiar.

There were about a dozen people on the pony trek, and most of them were children, which made another new experience for Dimanche, who was quite unused to being with other children. Valburga hated children, and Dimanche had never had a single friend to tea, for the simple reason that she hadn't got any friends. Even if she had, by some miracle, managed to meet another child, Valburga would never have allowed her to invite anyone home to play.

Being with ten or so other children, varying in age from six to sixteen, was quite an eye-opener for Dimanche. At first she felt dreadfully shy, and went bright red when any of them spoke to her. They thought it odd that, at the age of nine, she should still have her nanny with them. Some of them thought it pretty odd that she should have had a nanny in the first place, even one as glamorous as Polly Pugh, who looked so gallant on a horse, and joined in all the games.

Gradually, though, Dimanche found herself getting used to the others, and they to her. Each evening they pitched their tents and hobbled their horses, and then, with Polly in charge, cooked wonderful meals over their camp fires. After supper Polly would fish her little silver harmonica out of her pocket and play strange, sad tunes on it, while the horses stamped and snorted, and the wind blew through the trees. Now and then an owl would hoot, off in the dark woods, and then the children would take turns at telling ghost stories.

It was one of Dimanche and Polly's happiest holidays. It was very nearly their last.

Seven

At the beginning of the summer that Dimanche was ten, her aunt dropped a bombshell. She was sitting at the big old dining table opposite Polly Pugh, eating her breakfast. Dimanche had finished and gone upstairs to make her bed.

"I was thinking of taking Dimanche deep-sea diving this summer, in Cardigan Bay, Madam," Polly said, "if it's all right with you. You did express an interest in her learning, and I've saved nearly enough money from my wages. I'm sure she would enjoy it, she's such an adventurous girl. And one ought to encourage such qualities in a child, don't you think?"

"I don't think anything about children ought to be encouraged!" snapped Valburga.

"But Madam, surely you agree that adventure brings out the best in children?" Polly persisted.

"Children don't want bringing out, Miss Pugh, any more than they want encouraging. What children want is squashing down! What children want is flattening out! And it is with this in mind, my dear, my valued, my esteemed Miss Pugh, that I've decided to give YOU the sack. Dimanche is off to boarding school. So there won't be any summer holiday this summer. Holidays are over, Miss Pugh. Pack your bags. Your services are no longer required."

Poor Polly Pugh. Tears splashed from both her eyes. Her nose clogged up, her cheeks turned blotchy, and her long thin fingers shook. "No, Madam, NO!" she cried. "Don't send my Dimanche away, she's much too young."

"Nonsense! And anyway, she's not your Dimanche."

"But Madam! There's no need! And think of the expense."

Desperation made Polly clever. She knew her boss hated spending money on Dimanche, even though it was Dimanche's money she was spending.

"After all, Madam," she continued, "I can educate the child myself. In fact I am. We have already read *Hamlet*, and *A Midsummer Night's Dream*, and we're halfway through *Macbeth* at this very moment. Dimanche knows the whole of Lord Macaulay's *Horatius* and all her tables, including her seven and her nine times, which you know are the two worst. She can add and take away and multiply and divide. She can do fractions and contractions. She can name and identify twenty-seven species of ladybird. She can tell a swift from a swallow and a blackcap from a whitethroat. Really, Madam, the last thing Dimanche needs is any more education."

Poor Polly Pugh. If you love somebody, really love them, as she loved Dimanche, it's a terrible thing to see them in someone else's power. And when that person doesn't care for them at all, doesn't want what is best for them, isn't even interested in what happens to them, provided it's unpleasant – well, it's more than a human heart can bear. That was the situation Polly Pugh found herself in that breakfast time, and nothing she could do or say would change Valburga's mind. Dimanche must go away to school and Polly must be sacked.

"I can't think why you're objecting," scolded Valburga. "Dole on the Wold is a delightful school and it offers exactly the sort of education I require for Dimanche. The prospectus says they specialise in difficult children."

"But Dimanche isn't difficult! She's an angel."

"Don't be ridiculous, Miss Pugh! She's wayward, impetuous, untidy, disobedient, ill-mannered, annoying, and worst of all she's here, under my feet. I want her educated, and I want it done a long way away."

It seemed that no amount of arguing and pleading on Polly's part would change Valburga's mind. Dimanche tried her hardest to be brave when Polly broke the news to her. "I'll write to you, Polly," she promised. "And you must write to me. Where will you go, Polly?"

"I haven't thought. I can't imagine. I simply and utterly just don't know," Polly replied. "Pass me a paper hankie, there's a pet. Good heavens, is the box empty already?"

The next few evenings were spent sadly sewing Cash's name tapes on to Dimanche's new school clothes. Valburga went up to Harrods specially to buy them.

The cost displeased her a great deal, but she was glad to see that they looked both ugly and uncomfortable.

Dimanche's uniform was a prickly grey skirt that stuck to her legs when she sat down in it, and a maroon jumper with a v-neck which went over a stiff white shirt. It wasn't just the colours that were horrid, either. The skirt was baggy before she'd even put it on, and the collar of the shirt was so stiff that once you'd put it on you could only look straight ahead. The pièce de résistance was a tie which Dimanche couldn't tie, in maroon and mustard, with a black zigzag down it like the pattern you find on an adder's back. There were also heavy black lace-up shoes which reminded Polly of the boots divers wear to stop them floating to the surface of the water. And into every sock, and every vest, every pair of pants (scratchy and grey), into every beastly garment, Dimanche and Polly had to sew a name tape. It was dismal work.

They had finished underclothes and were halfway through shirts when Dimanche stuck her needle into the arm of her chair and cleared her throat. "Polly," she said, "I'm not going. I won't go. And she can't make me go."

"Do you know, Dimanche," Polly answered, "that's just exactly what I've decided too."

"What shall we do, Polly?"

"I'm not sure yet. But I've got an old great aunt – a nice one, not like yours at all – who lives forty or so miles from here as the crow flies. We'll go to her. She'll hide us till we work out what to do next."

Eight

That night Dimanche and Polly packed a few belongings – tent, compass, Ordnance Survey maps, cooking pots, camping stove, sleeping bags, mackintoshes, dry socks, clean underpants, toothbrushes, sunflower seeds and a good supply of dried apricots.

They waited till the grandfather clock at the bottom of the wide stone staircase had struck midnight, and the light under Valburga's door was out. Cyclops had slunk away through the rose garden to the rabbit warren which he liked to plunder in the spring, when the young rabbits were slow and juicy, and foolish enough to walk into his mouth if he simply left it open. All the old house was asleep. The garden lay milky in the moonlight. Dimanche and Polly crept silently down the back stairs, through the dark kitchen, and out into the night.

They went first to the greenhouse, where they wrote a letter to Cosmo, telling him that they were running away to Polly's great aunt Angelica, and giving him the great aunt's address so that he could write to them there.

EAT THIS MESSAGE WHEN YOU'VE READ IT,

Dimanche printed at the bottom of the note.

"D'you think you ought to put that?" Polly asked. "He might really do it, you know. He's awfully fond of you."

"He's quite fond of you too," Dimanche said.

But she added a PS:

OR BURY IT, IF YOU PREFER. JUST DON'T LET THE OLD BANGER SEE IT.
LOVE AND KISSES, DIMANCHE.

The old banger was their name for Valburga. They hid the letter inside the cold frame, where Cosmo was sure to see it when he watered the radishes, and the old banger was sure not to, because she never did.

Then they slipped away across the moonlit lawns, along the path Cosmo kept smooth and close-mown between the avenue of yew trees, flitting like two small ghosts through the soft spring air. They scrambled over the ha-ha at the bottom of the gardens and trotted away through the grove of damson trees Darcy had planted long ago in celebration of his marriage to Dolores.

If anyone had been watching, they might have caught a last glimpse of something shining like water – it was Polly's long red hair – and a last flicker of Dimanche's dark curls, before the two fugitives disappeared into the springtime countryside.

Dimanche needed every ounce of her tenacity that night just to keep going, out of moonlight into darkness, out of bush into bog and back into bracken, under trees and over fences, loaded down every step of the way with essential equipment. She did not once say: "Did we have to bring all this stuff?" Or, "I'm tired, can't we stop for a bit?" She just put one foot in front of the other, kept her head down, and walked.

They skirted round that part of the woods where the travelling people stayed, because their dogs would hear anyone passing near to the camp. They were friendly enough people, and knew Dimanche from her car-cleaning days. But Polly felt that the fewer people who saw them, the less chance the old banger would have of learning which way they'd gone.

"Are you sure she'll want to catch us, Polly?" Dimanche asked. "She doesn't like me. I should think she'd be glad if I disappeared."

Polly shook her head. She had guessed some time ago what her employer was up to but she had decided to put off telling Dimanche for as long as possible.

"It's my job to protect her, not to frighten her," she told herself, "and that is what I'll do." It hadn't always been easy.

Polly remembered with a shudder the narrow escape with the birthday bicycle. How could she forget it? The aunt had surprised both Polly and Dimanche very much indeed, the year she bought Dimanche a birthday present.

She had never done it before and she never did it again. But on this particular birthday she ordered a really stunning bicycle for Dimanche. It was a ten-speed racer with drop-handlebars and derailleur gears.

Its tyres were so fine they hardly touched the road. Its super-light alloy frame was painted in racing green and it had a bottle with a plastic straw on the handlebars as well as a five-tone battery-operated siren that played the noisy part of Tchaikovsky's 1812 Overture.

"Happy Birthday, Dimanche," Valburga said, and handed it over.

Dimanche was almost speechless with surprise, but she managed to stammer out a thank you.

"I suggest you take it to the top of Steepdown Hill, and test it there. Don't wait for Miss Pugh, I sent her to the Post Office. She will probably be ages – you know how Gussie Godiva can talk."

So Dimanche had wobbled off happily in the direction her aunt had suggested. It was a long, hard push out of the village and up to the top of Steepdown Hill, but once there the view was spectacular. Brown and yellow fields, clumps of dark woodland, the shining curve of the Fenny Water, and far in the distance the silver line of estuary and sea. Swinging one leg up and over and pushing off with the other, Dimanche began to freewheel down the hill.

At first it felt wonderful. Cool air blew in her face, and the hedges and ditches peeled past on either side.

The elegant new wheels whirled, the silver spokes thrummed, and Dimanche told herself that her aunt must finally have turned over a new leaf.

Dimanche was new to cycling, but it wasn't long before she realised that she was travelling too fast. Carefully she squeezed the brakes. Gently at first. Then harder. Nothing happened. She used all the power in her small hands. Still nothing By this time Dimanche's teeth were rattling in her jaw and her fingers ached from holding on so tightly. She forced herself to look straight ahead at the broad expanse of the river. The water looked deep and cold but Dimanche knew what she must do. She hung on till she was almost at the bottom of the hill, then swung her handlebars a fraction to the left. Child and machine left the road, shot through the top of the hawthorn hedge, and hit the river at a speed of thirty miles per hour.

When you collide with water at this kind of speed it's a hard landing. The bicycle was smashed to bits which sank, bubbling, down on to the river bed. Dimanche herself plunged down under the green water. Her feet sank into the soft ooze on the bottom; opening her eyes for a second she saw the silver flick of a fin close by her cheek. Then she was rising, rushing upwards, gasping and spluttering. She trod water for a few moments, looking round hopefully for signs of her new bicycle. Then she struck out for the river bank.

There had been many times, Polly reflected as they crossed a small meadow full of ox-eye daisies, when without a good deal of luck as well as her own loving care, Dimanche would certainly have come to harm. Neither of them would ever forget the dreadful sound of breaking ice last winter. Valburga seemed so certain that the ice on the pond would hold. "I tested it myself this morning, before either of you were up," she said. "It's as sound as a bell."

If Polly had not insisted on tying a rope round Dimanche's waist before allowing her to skate, who knows what might have happened when the ice gave way?

The time has come, Polly thought, *when I must warn the child about the danger she's in*. She took a deep breath. "Let's rest here for a minute, Dimanche," she suggested. "We've done pretty well so far, though we're not out of the woods yet."

"We are," Dimanche pointed out. "That's the road to Rockford Market up ahead."

And there it was, a little country lane, pale in the

moonlight, with a lace edging of cow parsley stretching away on either side between bud-heavy hedges. Polly shook her head.

"That isn't what I meant. Dimanche, there's something I must talk to you about."

Sometimes, if you need to tell someone something bad, it's difficult to know just how to start. That's how it was for Polly. The two friends sat on the bank in silence. Polly leaned back into the hedge, and Dimanche leaned back into Polly, and neither of them spoke. A moth flew by, drawn by the scent of flowers in the hedge. Polly watched it for a moment, then sat up and turned Dimanche round to face here.

"Your aunt will catch us if she can, Dimanche."

"You said that, Polly, but I don't know why. She doesn't like me. Why should she want me back?"

"She doesn't want *you*, Dimanche. She wants the money you'll inherit on your eighteenth birthday."

"Will I get money, Polly? Enough for us to go on holiday again?"

"Much more than that. You will inherit a fortune, Dimanche. You will be a very rich young woman on your eighteenth birthday."

"How do you know?"

"I steamed open a letter from the bank."

"Polly, you didn't!"

"I had to know if I was right in my suspicions."

"And you were?"

"Absolutely. On your eighteenth birthday, Dimanche, you will inherit Hilton Hall and all its lands and its estates – that's all the woods and fields – as well as several million pounds."

Dimanche felt quite giddy with excitement. She had had no idea that she would ever be anything but rather poor. The only money she was used to was pocket money Polly gave her from her wages, and what she'd earned by washing cars. Several million pounds was far more than she could imagine. And the whole house! And all the woods and fields!

"Your parents were very rich," Polly went on. "And you are their sole heir. There are no other living Dillers, apart from your aunt. All she has to do is wait until your eighteenth birthday, Dimanche, and then force you to give the money over to her."

"She couldn't do that, Polly."

"She might find a way. And there's something worse. Something you may as well face now. If you were to die, Dimanche, who do you think would get your money?"

"HER?"

The moonlight polished Polly's red hair and made dark shadows under her large eyes. "That's who, my pet."

It was at that moment that they heard, coming down the lane from Rockford Market direction, the slow clip-clop of hooves on tarmac, and the steady creak of wheels.

Nine

Polly and Dimanche hid behind the hedge and peered out at the little empty lane. Presently a glimmer of grey appeared. It was moonlight shining on a pale mane which nodded in time to the clop of four shod hooves on the road.

An old roan pony separated herself gradually from the night-time shadows. She was pulling a covered cart – not the sort you might see parked outside a pub with flowers growing round it, or on one of those pretend farms they have in country parks. No. This was a plainish cart, with wooden sides, and what must have been wooden hoops, willow perhaps, slotted into the sides. Over them was stretched a hood of patched and mended canvas. It may have had a colour once, but that was long since bleached away by summer sun and winter frost. The back, though Dimanche and Polly could not see it yet, was laced shut like a tent. The front was undone. The oval shape of its opening made a dark frame for the little figure who sat there, wrapped in a thick coat and staring straight ahead between the pricked ears of the pony.

When the pony drew level with the place where Dimanche and Polly crouched behind the hedge, she stopped and swung her heavy head towards them. She lowered her nose and snuffed as though she was saying hello. Dimanche wanted to say hello back, and pull up a handful of grass and step out on to the road and feel the tickly softness of that old nose on the palm of her hand, but Polly nudged her gently and put a finger to her lips. The two of them stayed perfectly still, bent over in the grass behind the hedge, not moving, not speaking, as still as two fence posts.

"Evening," the person on the cart said.

Dimanche stood up. It seemed only polite. "How did you see us?" she asked.

"My sharp eyes showed me, Miss, where you was hiding in the hedge."

"Who are you?"

The man on the cart pulled a pipe out of his pocket. He filled it, and tamped it down, and lit it, all before answering. A sweet twist of pipe smoke floated in soft circles of blue between himself and the two figures by the hedge.

"My name is Marmara," he said. "My name is Valparaiso. My name is Rhadamanthys. My name is Papa Fettler and Papa Vittler. My name is Long Tom, though I'm short of stature. I am a travelling man."

A little silence followed this announcement. Into that silence crept the regular squeak of something mechanical coming down the road from the direction of Hilton Hall. Dimanche knew instantly what it was. Only the Banger's bicycle squeaked in just that way. Dimanche looked up at the old man, still sitting in the open door frame of his covered cart. His bright eyes shone under the brim of his hat as he smiled down at her.

"Care to step up?" he asked. "I do believe that be your aunt a-coming down the road aboard her bicycle.

Not a pretty sight. And looking for you and your good friend Polly Pugh, I'm certain. I do advise you to step up quickly."

"Thank you, Papa Fettler," Dimanche whispered. It was the only one of his names that had stuck in her mind. She glanced round at Polly who was standing stock still behind her. Polly hesitated a second, then nodded, and the two of them scrambled up on to the shafts of the cart, squeezed past Papa Fettler, and dived into the dark interior of the caravan.

Dark was the word. Velvet dark, moleskin dark, play-with-the-gypsies-in-the-wood dark. There seemed to be some sort of rug on the floor, and a dark bed like a little shelf running down one side. Dimanche and Polly did not explore. They huddled together on the floor, not daring to move, not even when something warm and wet reached out and licked Dimanche on the nose, and something thin and whippy thumped against Polly's cheek.

Outside, the bicycle squeak grew louder, and stopped. Valburga's voice spoke only inches away from Dimanche's ears.

"I'm looking for my niece, old fellow. Have you seen her? Speak up, my man."

"Your niece, my lady? Now wouldn't that be little Dimanche Diller? A sweet child, as I recall, and loved by all who've seen her."

"Doesn't sound anything like my niece, you batty old fool. She's a spoilt scrawny bit of a brat. Dark hair. Dirty face. Usually up to no good. She will be travelling with an ex-employee of mine, an irresponsible young woman who has abducted her. Made off with her. Don't ask me why. So here I am, long after midnight, wearing my fingers to the bone searching high and low to find the two of them and bring my niece back home to Hilton Hall where she belongs. Have you seen either of them?"

"No, Madam. Not a smidgen, not a pigeon. Not one jot nor tittle of 'em."

"Are you certain?"

"Madam. Do I look like an uncertain sort of person?"

"Yes. And if find that you've seen them and not told me, I'll have you turned off my land and out of my woods and very likely into my river."

"I understand, Madam, that land, wood, river, field and fortune all belong to little Dimanche."

"And where d'you think she'd be without an aunt like me to look after them for her?"

"That I don't know, Madam. No more than you know where she bes with you."

"I'm not standing here listening to you a second longer, you daft old cuss! I don't know what's come over me, to stand here at all! If you do see them, send word to me at Hilton Hall, or it'll be the worse for you."

"Good night, Madam. A pleasant journey to you."

Valburga snorted, turned her bicycle round, hauled herself aboard it and squeaked and wobbled back down the road towards Hilton Hall. Papa Fettler clicked with his tongue and old Rosie lifted her head, leaned into the collar of her harness, and with steady steps pulled the little caravan away down the lane.

Ten

When the squeak of the bicycle had faded away to nothing, Papa Fettler spoke over his shoulder into the dark interior of the cart.

"Don't let Jack startle you, Miss Dimanche. Nor you, Miss Polly. He's a good dog. A Jack-be-nimble sort of dog, light of foot and long-nosed. I dare say he's said good evening to you already, has he?"

"Yes," Dimanche answered. "He licked my face!"

"That shows he likes you. He'd have bit your

ankle otherwise."

"Are you sure she's gone?" Polly asked. "She's not following us, is she? Only she didn't seem entirely to believe you, did she, Papa Fettler? Or should I call you Papa Vittler? Or was it – was it Valparaiso?"

"No. She's not following us. Jack would have told me if she was. You would have heard his bark or whine. But that don't mean she won't follow. I'll put a mile or two between her and us, before I set you down."

"Thank you," Polly said, "we'd be very glad of that."

"How do you know us?" Dimanche asked. "You know who we are and everything about us, but I've never seen you before. Not in the woods, or with the travellers, or anywhere around. And I've lived here for ages."

"How many ages, Miss Dimanche?"

"Nearly ten years. Almost all my life."

"Almost all your life is long. Couldn't be much longer, could it? But I was here a while before that."

"Are we going past the post box?" Polly asked. "Because if we are, I'd like to post a letter to Chief Superintendent Barry Bullpit. He's the policeman who took charge of Dimanche when she was a baby."

The old man nodded. "After that we'll turn off for Rockford Market. Best to keep the back closed up until we're well on the other side of the village, to be on the safe side. I like to be on the safe side of what I can be, and on the far side of what I can't."

They jogged along without talking after that. Dimanche slept, lying on the rug with her head on Polly's lap and her feet against Jack's warm belly. She did not wake until daylight shone through the thin canvas and lit the inside of Papa Fettler's caravan. She sat up then, and found she'd been tucked into the little bunk bed, with a blanket wrapped round her. Jack ran behind now, and Polly had moved up to the front where she sat proudly holding the reins. Papa Fettler walked along beside the pony. They seemed to be talking to one another.

The inside of the caravan was very tidy, except for Polly and Dimanche's own belongings – the tent, the sleeping bags, the pots and pans and all the rest, which they'd been carrying on their backs, and which were now pushed in under a little table.

Dimanche got up, smoothed down her hair with her fingers, and went to sit by Polly.

"Can I hold the reins?" she asked. Polly nodded, and handed them over.

The day passed in a dream of green fields and hedges, small farms, woods, and villages, all of which went by so slowly that there was time to look at everything for as long as you wanted to. And when you'd looked long enough at one thing, there was always another. They had bread and cheese and beer for lunch, and Papa Fettler said they'd have mushrooms on toast for supper, if they happened to stop in a place where they grew. Polly's Great Aunt Angelica lived about thirty miles the other side of Rockford Market. If Papa Fettler took them to the little town, Polly felt that she and Dimanche could walk the rest of the way, taking their time, and camping by night.

Late in the afternoon thick rain clouds rolled across the sky. By supper-time a hard, cold rain was falling, soaking poor Rosie and pattering and spattering off the canvas roof. It drenched Papa Fettler in spite of the waterproof cape and sou'wester he took from under his seat. He spread an old tarpaulin over Rosie's back and, turning off the road, led her down a track between high hedges to an old barn beside a stretch of the Fenny Water.

"We'll stop here for the night," Papa Fettler said. "My Rosie must have shelter in weather like this. You come and help me rub her down, Dimanche. Perhaps Polly Pugh will be so good as to forage in the cupboard for some dinner meanwhile. It's not mushrooming weather, I'm afraid."

Rosie plodded in through the open door as if she knew just what to expect, and Dimanche could see, on glancing round the barn, that this must be one of Papa Fettler's regular stopping places. There was a bale of dry straw in one corner, and a sack of oats in another with an empty bucket beside it.

"Water from the river, oats from the sack, and a good rub down is what a pony needs this weather," Papa Fettler said. He showed Dimanche how to twist up a handful of straw into a sort of brush, and rub Rosie's wet coat, round and round and up and down. Dimanche worked on her legs, and Papa Fettler did her back, making a hissing sound through his teeth while he did so. When the pony's coat was drying nicely, Papa Fettler threw a blanket over her back and gave her food and drink before saying goodnight. "We'll come back and see her in a while," he said. "A pony her age, which is more than twice yours, could take a chill easy, on a night like this. There's been times when I've lit her a fire in here, on winter nights when frost was sharp or snow lay deep."

Inside the caravan, Polly had lit the little iron stove and was cutting up onions, potatoes and carrots to make soup. Papa Fettler took a bottle of beer from under the seat and divided it between three mugs. Dimanche didn't like beer, it tasted sour to her and smelt worse, but she drank it anyway so as not to be rude.

"We'll talk while the soup's cooking," Papa Fettler said. "About your aunt."

"Must we?" asked Dimanche. "I don't think I want to."

Off in the night a lone dog barked. Jack twitched in his sleep at Papa Fettler's feet. The sound of rain drumming on the canvas roof was cosy.

"We must," Papa Fettler insisted. "It's my belief that there's a mystery connected with that aunt of yours, Dimanche. And I'd say that you most likely hold the key to it."

"Me?"

"Yes indeed. Keys are easy lost, but all that's lost may yet be found. And there are things you may remember that could point us the way."

"Are there, Papa Fettler? Are you sure?"

"Certain. Think back, child. Back to when you were a little sprig of a cricket, back as far back as you can, and then back. Open your mind and let yourself float free on memory's brook."

Dimanche gazed up at Papa Fettler's weather-beaten face. Her grey eyes shone, his gentle voce soothed her fears away, and as she listened, she felt herself growing smaller, younger, lighter. The drumming of the rain on canvas faded. The tug and flap of the night wind, the occasional stamp and rustle of Rosie in the barn, Jack worriting for fleas in his sleep – she heard them still, but from a great way off.

Closer by she heard bees buzzing, and seemed to see light filtering down through soft green leaves. Daisies grew in the grass all round her, daisies lay in the lap of her summer dress. It was the one with bluebirds on it, the one Sister Sophia had made her just before she had to go away. Behind the buzzing of the bees Dimanche could hear the sound of digging, and Old Tom Shovel the gravedigger talking, talking, in a sort of rhyme.

"Sweet as a nut your auntie used to be,
I never saw a body change as much as she.
Changes a-plenty Old Tom Shovel seen,
But if that be your auntie, I'm the fairy queen."

Dimanche must have repeated Old Tom Shovel's words out loud, because Papa Fettler was nodding his head. "I thought so," he said. "It doesn't surprise me one bit."

"What did you think?" Dimanche asked. She felt as if she'd been asleep. "What doesn't surprise you, Papa Fettler?"

"That aunt of yours is not the real thing," he said. "And Tom Shovel knew it. He will have known your real auntie, long ago. He's a might mysterious man, is Tom Shovel. Gravediggers often are, you'll find. It comes of their calling."

"So my aunt's really an impostor?" Dimanche asked. Papa Fettler nodded. "Then we must go back to Hilton in the Hollow and ask Mr Shovel to tell us everything he knows."

"Are you sure we must, Dimanche?" asked Polly. "Shouldn't we go on to my great aunt Angelica's, as we planned? We could write to Tom Shovel from there."

"No! We must go straight to Mr Shovel's cabin," Dimanche said. "Think of it, Polly! I might have a real aunt somewhere! A real relation."

Polly knew how much this idea meant to Dimanche. "All right," she agreed. "We'll do it. But we must not get caught."

Papa Fettler thought for a moment. Then he reached under the seat and pulled out an old leather bag. "This calls for disguises," he said.

By the time Papa Fettler had finished, Polly Pugh and Dimanche Diller had disappeared entirely. In Polly's place sat a young travelling woman, her dark hair hanging down in plaits and her brown skin shining with seasons spent outside. She wore a man's coat, tied round her middle with a bit of string, and a billowing skirt. On her head was a soft felt hat decorated with jays' feathers. Beside her sat a little boy of nine or ten. His skin was stained brown by sun, wind and dirt, and his short hair curled round his face. His trousers were faded and his shoes were split. His jacket looked as though it had been handed down a chain of older brothers and reached him well before it should have done – if he turned the collar up it hid half his face, and the sleeves hung down over his hands.

"Will we do, Papa Fettler?" asked the boy.

"You will. I'd like to come with you, but me and my Rosie are too well known. I'll send Jack with you. If you want me, he'll fetch me. Sleep now. I'll take a look at Rosie, see that all's well with her, and join you."

Eleven

Dimanche and Polly, disguised as a travelling woman and her little son, crept into the village of Hilton in the Hollow late the next evening. They had taken their time walking back, stopping here and there to sell clothes pegs and other useful things which Papa Fettler had provided in order to make their disguise convincing.

"Of course," he said, "it wouldn't fool anybody as really knows you, but it will serve to put the false aunt off your trail."

They learnt a great deal about what sort of people are polite to travellers and what sort are not, that day, and they walked a lot further than Dimanche wanted to. But at least this time they were not carrying tent, cooking pots, sleeping bags, and all the rest of their gear. They left all that with Papa Fettler, and arranged to meet him in the woods after they'd spoken to Tom Shovel. "If you need me urgently, send Jack on. He'll find his way to me. And I shall find mine to you, never fear," he told them.

Tom Shovel's little house was on the outskirts of the village, close by the church. He had built it himself, and lived there all alone. The walls were made of clay, and the roof was made of corrugated iron, and there was a vegetable garden at the front and a flower garden at the back – "Because that's how I like it," Tom would say.

Dimanche crept up to the back of the house with Polly close behind her. It took her a moment to get up enough courage to tap on the door. Tom Shovel was, as Papa Fettler said, a mysterious sort of person, perhaps not the sort of person you'd choose to visit late at night. From his bedroom he looked out over the graves he'd dug, and those his father had dug, and those his grandfather before him had dug.

If he saw any comings and goings in the churchyard at night he never told anyone. "Ain't you afraid to live close by the graves like that?" people would sometimes ask him.

"No," he'd reply. "Why should I be? Why should I fear the dead? Or ghosts? Or graves? To me they're company."

It seemed strange to Tom Shovel – folk were not afraid, after all, when a new baby was born in the village. They were glad then, crowding round pushchairs, peeping into prams, drawn into the joy and excitement of a new beginning. But at the other end of things, the goodbye end, Tom called it, they came over all of a tremble. No crowding round then. Not if folk could help it.

Tom dug his graves with care, and filled them in with respect, and never topped up a flower vase with fresh water or pulled up dandelions from the smooth green mounds without remembering who lay beneath, and wondering if they'd gone on to another sort of life, or if the grave was their full-stop. People were uncomfortable with him because death was his business. Even people as sensible as Dimanche and Polly had to pause on his back doorstep to get their courage up before they knocked on his door.

They heard him push his chair back, scraping the legs across the brick floor of his kitchen, and the slow clump of his boots as he crossed the room. The door creaked open a little way, candlelight shone out, and Tom Shovel's silhouette stood up tall and black against the bright inside of the kitchen.

"Who's that then?" he asked. "Somebody died, have they?"

"No," Dimanche answered. "It's us – Dimanche and Polly, from the big house. Can we talk to you, please, Mr Shovel?"

The door opened wider and a candle shone on to Dimanche's face. Tom Shovel smiled. "I wouldn't have known you, Miss Dimanche," he said. "Nor you, Miss Pugh. That's an excellent and thorough-going disguise. What's it in aid of? High jinks, is it? Come in and tell me. I see you've got Long Tom's dog there. Bring him in and all."

Inside, the kitchen was warm and dirty. Tom Shovel went round closing up his shutters and pulling his tattered curtains until he was sure nobody could see in. Then he put bread and jam and bitter black tea on the table. He broke a crust of bread off the loaf and gave it to Jack, who carried it under the table and chewed on it there.

He poured three mugs of tea and passed round bread and jam. Dimanche found it was quite hard to swallow the tea without making a face.

"Don't care for Tom Shovel's tea, eh?" Tom commented. "I'll fetch us out a drop of nettle wine then." Dimanche thought that might easily be nastier than bitter black tea, but when she tried it she found it was quite nice and tingly.

"Now then," Tom said, when they were settled. "What's going on? Why are you two gallivanting about the countryside at night dressed up as travelling people? And with Long Tom's dog in tow?"

Dimanche cleared her throat and began. "I'm not sure if I've remembered this, Mr Shovel," she said. "I may have dreamed it. But I think you told me something once – a little rhyme – about my aunt. Did you?"

Tom nodded. "You were sat in my graveyard, watching me dig, and making daisy chains. Not long after you first come to Hilton Hall. Such a cheerful child you were. I used to like to see you trotting down the lane into the churchyard, with one of your nurse-maids flouncing along behind you – I'm speaking about the time before your Polly Pugh come. I think there was only me and young Cosmo up at the big house who ever took much notice of you, back in them days. You didn't seem to have nobody on your side. Why you was so cheerful I don't know. Anyway, I told you what I knew. And I told it to you in a rhyme so's you'd remember it. Rhymes have a way of coming back to you when you least expect 'em. It's what they was invented for. Seemingly mine came back to you all right. Of which I'm mighty glad."

"It did, Mr Shovel. So please will you tell me everything you know and guess about my aunt? My real aunt?"

Twelve

"I will, and gladly, Miss Dimanche. I've waited a long time for you to knock on my door and ask that very question. Now you'll have to wait a bit while I answer it." Tom Shovel blew his nose, and eased his heavy boots off.

"Your Auntie Verity, your mother's sister, I'm going to speak of now. Lovely young thing she was – they both was. Your mum fell for your dad, didn't she?"

"I expect so," Dimanche agreed. "He looks smashing in his photos."

Tom Shovel nodded. "But your Auntie Verity, she fell in love with a Frenchy. Name of Valery Victorine. Nice feller. Handsome, and kind, and good – just the man for your Aunt Verity."

Tom was silent for a while, apart from the chewing noises he made with his bread and jam. "That crabby old baggage up at the big house ain't your aunt," he went on presently. "That nun's outfit don't fool me. I knew little Verity from when she was in her pram alongside your mother, and your grandma Britannia pushing them both out each morning through the village. They lived at one end of the village, your mum's people did, and your dad's at the other. Everyone was quite made up when they took to each other and got wed, your mum and dad."

"But if the old banger's not my aunt, where *is* my aunt, Mr Shovel? And who is the old banger?"

"Wait awhile. Don't be hasty. Tom'll make it all clear."

Tom sat in silence for a while, staring into his glass of nettle wine, before going on with his story.

"Your grandad, old Mr Bertram, was a mite stuck-up. Not what you'd call a forward-looking man, though not a bad one either. Old-fashioned, he was, and he wanted Verity to marry an Englishman.

Your grandma Britannia tried to make him see sense, but he wouldn't. So Verity up and run off to her Frenchman, and it's my belief your grandma helped her go. Women of your family's always been full of go. No one could hold 'em down. Off she run to France and married her Valery."

"Good," Polly sighed. "I bet they were blissfully happy."

"Well, they was, so far as I know," Tom Shovel said, "but not for long. Valery took a fever and died the very next year. He left poor little Verity alone, in a foreign land, with a broken heart and no money."

Tom put more wood on the fire, and bent to scratch old Jack behind the ear. He topped up the three glasses on the table with nettle wine and opened a packet of biscuits. Dimanche sat and thought of young Verity, alone, with a broken heart.

"What happened next?" she asked.

"Next," Tom replied, "your poor young aunt ran off to a convent to nurse her broken heart. Become a nun, she did, and wrote home to tell your grandma of it. Well. There was ructions then. Bad enough to marry a foreigner, your grandad thought. Worse to be left a widow. But to go into a nunnery, shut yourself away from the world, well, that was the bottom, your grandad thought. He was not a contemplative sort of man. Your grandma was that cut up she took to her bed and died. Your mum was proper shaken.

"She wrote back to her sister an angry sort of letter, and Verity, although she was a nun and all, wrote back an angrier one, and so it went on."

"Sisters," Polly sighed, tucking her plaits into her collar. "Why do they always have to fight?"

"They would have come to their senses," Tom said, "given time. But time is what they weren't given. Verity's last letter to your mum arrived here the very week you did, Miss Dimanche, in care of that wicked old party who says she's your aunt and isn't. Fell right into her hands."

"How awful! Do you know what it said?"

"I've got it here, Miss Dimanche. I found it where she threw it, down behind a gravestone. You can read it yourself." Tom Shovel creaked over to the corner cupboard and fetched an old brown envelope. Out of this he took one thin sheet of paper, which he passed to Dimanche.

Dearest Dolores, (Dimanche read aloud)

I beg you, let's put our quarrel behind us, let's be friends again. Won't you come and visit me, and see how lovely it is here, and try to understand the choice I've made? Please, please, please write back and say you forgive me, say we're friends again, if not for your own sake, then for the sake of your adorable little daughter, whom I long to see. Dearest Dolores, if after this I still hear no friendly words from you, I shall not write again. But I don't believe that's what you want. So write to me, dear Dolores.

Your loving sister –

Verity Victorine

Polly sniffed, and Dimanche wiped her eyes.

"How awful," she said quietly. "She got no answer. She didn't know that Mum was dead. She thought Mum didn't care. So she never wrote again."

"That's about it," Tom Shovel nodded. "She never even knew your mum had named you for her. You was born on a Sunday, see, and what with your mum's sister being off in France, she thought Dimanche would make a pretty name for you."

"I've always liked my name," Dimanche agreed. "But what's the banger's name, Mr Shovel? Do you know that?"

"Reckon I do. When I found your Auntie Verity's letter, crumpled up and stuck down the side of a headstone, I found some other bits and pieces, old papers that had been got rid of. They was addressed to someone whose initials was VV, but that VV didn't stand for Verity Victorine. I seen the name in full, it was Valburga Vilemile. I reckon that's the name that belongs with your old baggage up at the big house."

Dimanche thought for a while. "But if you knew all this, Mr Shovel, why didn't you tell someone?" she asked.

"I'm not a hasty man. By the time I'd made up my mind to do something, your Polly Pugh was here. Well, once she came, I could see that you was safe and loved. So I thought, in time, she'll come to me, and when she does it will be time enough to tell her."

"I see," said Dimanche, although she didn't, exactly. "But all this time, my poor Aunt Verity has been waiting for one kind word from my mother."

"Aye, she has that," Tom agreed. "But I expect you'll make it up to her."

"I certainly will. I'll write at once to the address at the top of her letter."

"I wouldn't trust the post, Miss Dimanche."

"Why ever not?"

"I've a feeling that Valburga Vilemile is in league with the post mistress, Gussie Godiva. I wouldn't feel comfortable in my bones that your letter would find its way to your real aunt, not if you posted it."

"How can I get it to her then?"

"Buy many onions, do you?" Tom asked.

"Onions?" asked Dimanche. "No, I don't. But can't we finish talking about my letter before we talk about onions?"

"Your letter is what I'm talking about, when I say onions."

"Papa Fettler said you were mysterious."

"He's a fine one to talk. He's got more names than an onion has skins."

"My letter, Mr Shovel."

"Yes, Miss. The French onion man is in the village, staying with the schoolmaster, I believe. Tomorrow he'll sell the last of his onions, and then he'll be off home. With your letter in his pocket, if you like.

He's an old friend of mine. Perhaps you'd better write your letter now, and then I'll find you both somewhere to sleep."

Thirteen

In the morning, Dimanche took out her letter and read it over to make sure she'd said everything she wanted to say.

Dearest real Aunt Verity, (she had written)

This letter will be a big surprise for you. I hope the part about me will be a nice one.
I hope you are well and like being a nun. I am well.

My mum and dad were both drowned when I was a baby. It's very sad I know, but try not to be too upset. I have a real friend here, her name is Polly Pugh and she looks after me, but we are On the Run. We need you to come home as soon as possible to prove Valburga Vilemile isn't you.

Please come.

This is URGENT.

Lots of love from Dimanche Diller.

PS   Come first to Mr Shovel the gravedigger's house, beside the churchyard. We will try to get a message to you there.

Love again, Dimanche.

PPS Please hurry.

Tom Shovel found an envelope and sealed it with a blob of red sealing wax, and he took it to the onion man at the schoolmaster's house. He said Dimanche and Polly shouldn't risk being seen in the village, even in disguise, unless they had to.

"D'you think the onion man will deliver my letter, Polly?" Dimanche asked. Now that she knew about her, she couldn't wait to be united with Verity Victorine.

"No doubt about it, pet. He'll reach Dover by tomorrow, I dare say, and cross the Channel the same day. Your proper aunt will be reading your letter, and crying her eyes out, and packing her bags, by the day after. You and me will hide away safe with Papa Fettler till she gets here. And don't forget I wrote to Chief Superintendent Bullpit to put him in the picture too."

"What did you say?"

"I said I feared the old banger was up to no good and asked him to check up on her."

"D'you think he will?"

"Sure to. I wouldn't be surprised if he didn't turn up here very shortly and make some enquiries on the spot."

Later on that morning Tom Shovel went out to see who was about in the village. Nobody was, except for Cyclops, dozing on the churchyard wall. "You'll get no scraps from me, you old bloat," Tom told him.

"You hunt your own dinner. Or else ask Her for some." The cat said nothing, of course, but he looked at Tom Shovel's cottage in a knowing sort of way.

Ten minutes later Dimanche and Polly, with Jack trotting beside them, came out of Tom Shovel's little cabin and made their way though the churchyard and out across the fields. It was a still, warm day, and the scent of hawthorn blossom was almost sickly. Waist-high grass and flowers formed a tunnel over Jack's head so that all you could see of his progress was the waving tops of the grasses. Off at the edges of the fields a cuckoo called, its two-note song floating back to Dimanche and Polly as though down a tunnel. How do they make that noise? Dimanche wondered. And why don't we ever see them? And *why* don't they make nests of their own? She felt too hot, but didn't want to remove any part of her disguise. Polly may have guessed some of what Dimanche was thinking. She didn't say anything about cuckoos, but she did say that once they were deep in the woods they'd stop to rest, and eat the food Tom Shovel had given them.

Both of them felt safer once they reached the shelter of the trees. Behind them the valley of Hilton in the Hollow lay like a cup of light. Ahead was the wood, dark and cool and green. Pigeons paced up and down the branches of tall oak trees, cooing and bowing to one another.

Jack ran on, snuffing here and there. A hen pheasant rose from her nest with a whirr. She need not have bothered to fly, for Jack was not in the hunting mood. He was busy snuffing out the route to Papa Fettler. Every now and then he'd flop down and pant, as dogs do when they're hot, until Dimanche and Polly caught up with him. At about what would have been teatime if they'd had any tea, Dimanche noticed the trees were growing further apart, letting the light dapple through, and a sparkle caught her eye. She ran on ahead of Polly and found a stream, not deep enough to swim in but good enough for cooling off.

"Just the place to stop and rest," Polly said, coming up beside her. "Shoes off, we'll cool our feet and eat our rations." Shoes were not enough for Dimanche. She removed almost everything – it felt so good to be rid of the heavy boy's clothes that Papa Fettler had disguised her in. She liked her short hair, it kept her neck cool. But she felt glad she was a girl, and could wear a dress when she wanted to. Papa Fettler had dyed her skin brown with something he'd boiled up, but he'd only dyed the bits that would show. Now that she had her jeans and jumper off, her white bits looked whiter than ever.

"You look like a dappled deer," Polly said, unlacing her boots and rolling up her heavy skirt. She sank her feet into the water and Dimanche sat down beside her and fanned her with a bit of bracken. Jack shut his eyes and put his head on his paws. Only his ears still twitched, to show he was on guard.

"I could stay here for ever," Polly said presently.

"Me too," Dimanche agreed. "We could live on nuts and berries and build ourselves a tree house. Let's."

"One day, Dimanche, we could do that for our summer holiday. Would you like that? Just camp out in the woods? Sleep on bracken beds in a hut made of branches? Shall we?"

"Yes, Polly! Definitely! Next summer! It wouldn't even cost much."

"Hardly a bean," Polly answered. "But for now, we must get up, and put our hot scratchy clothes back on, and walk."

Jack took them at a steady pace through woods and fields, across country lanes, and round the outside of two villages. Once they saw an old mother badger rolling along through a tunnel of fern, her broad back swaying from side to side, her long striped face nodding, and behind her, three cubs, their grey backs softer, fluffier, closer to the ground than hers, the stripes on their faces new-painted and sharp. Jack grunted, and dropped to the ground. Polly and Dimanche stood stock still and held their breath while the family trundled by, the old mother seeming to see them, and seeming not to care.

In the evening they rested again. "I should think we're no more than five miles at the most from where we're meeting Papa Fettler," Polly said. "What shall we do, Dimanche? Curl up here and sleep in the woods? Or go on a little, and try to find Papa Fettler tonight?"

Dimanche looked round and wondered. The woods seemed to have changed since they crossed the stream. Here yew trees, their poisonous berries winking like drops of blood, gloomed in the twilight. Beeches and oaks had been replaced by fir trees, and no pigeons cooed and courted in their branches. A stench of fox fouled the air. Or was it tom cat?

"I'd rather go on, Polly," she said. "I don't much like it here."

Polly nodded. "That's fine by me, Dimanche," she said. But fine, alas, it wasn't.

Fourteen

Dimanche was bending down to tie up her shoelaces when she caught a glimpse of something horrid falling out of a tree. At the same moment a familiar voice whipped across the darkness.

"Keep absolutely still, Dimanche Diller! And you, Polly Pugh! Don't move. Don't speak. Don't do a thing unless I tell you. I've got a pistol and I'm not afraid of using it."

"Don't be ridiculous, Madam…" Polly began.

A deafening explosion cut her words short and a shower of cream and pearly feathers tumbled through the air. A solitary barn owl had met its death to prove Valburga's point.

"How could you do that?" Dimanche gasped. "You really are a vile person! You could never be my real aunt."

"So you've found that out, have you? It took you long enough. And it's much too late for your discovery to do you any good. I could kill you every bit as easily as I killed that owl. In fact I'd rather like to. You're nothing but a spoilt brat."

"You have no right to speak to Dimanche like that!" Polly shouted. "And don't think that you'll get away with holding us prisoner, Valburga Vilemile!"

"Who's going to stop me?"

"Chief Superintendent Barry Bullpit for one! He's probably on his way here with a warrant for your arrest right now!"

"I doubt it. I read your letter. And your spelling is atrocious."

Poor Polly hung her head. Her letter had fallen into the wrong hands. (And it was quite true, she couldn't spell at all.) Help was not on the way after all.

Jack was their only hope now, and he was struggling under the weight of Cyclops, dodging needle-sharp claws and trying to get his teeth round the cat's neck. Luckily for him, courage was not Cyclops's strong point. He had used up most of his by jumping out of the tree. He was frightened of Valburga – that was why he was helping her. But he was more frightened of Jack's teeth, and of his gargling growl. He pulled his claws in, let Jack go, and shinned up a tree. Jack looked up at him just once, before scooting away through the wood.

"So much for your guard dog," Valburga snorted. "Now, get going. I intend to be in my bed by midnight. These spring nights can be chilly. It will be some time before either of you finds a warm bed, though."

"Where are you taking us?" Dimanche asked.

"Somewhere nobody will find you. Walk!"

Dimanche and Polly walked hand in hand and Valburga Vilemile followed just behind them with her pistol in her hand. Now and then she grunted instructions such as "Left past those hollies", or "Right before the fallen tree". Both prisoners wondered what their chances would be if they tried to run away, but then they remembered the thump of the barn owl's body hitting the ground, and the little puff of pearly feathers.

After what felt like ten miles, but was in face less than one, they reached the edge of the wood. On top of a hillock they saw a pile of mossy stones out of which grew nettles and brambles and one stunted bush. Pushing painfully through these and stepping over the trunk of a fallen tree, they came to a flight of steps which led down into the earth.

"Down you go!" Valburga ordered.

It was horribly dank and dark. Dimanche guessed that they were descending into what must be the cellar of her grandfather's old hunting lodge. All that was left of the house were the piles of stones above. Dimanche could make out dead leaves, and moss, and water dripping on to ferns. The place smelled of damp, but nothing worse. Still holding Polly's hand, she turned to face Valburga and her pistol.

"What have you brought us here for?" she asked.

"Don't you like it here? I think it's rather pleasant myself. But what you think about it doesn't matter. You're staying anyway."

Dimanche stood still half way down the steps. Everything about the place said TRAP, and she felt that if she went on down she might never see daylight again. She turned back to Polly, one step up behind her.

As she did so, Valburga Vilemile darted down the steps, her long nun's habit swishing round her ankles. She put all her weight behind a shove that sent Polly cannoning into Dimanche, knocking both of them down on to the floor of the cellar below. They landed in a huddle, and before either of them could get to their feet something heavy rolled across the opening above their heads and the cellar turned bible black.

Fifteen

Dimanche was first back up the steps. Her head hit something hard and she sat back down, tears stinging her eyes. Polly heard her beginning to cry and scrambled up beside her. She crouched down on the slimy steps and put her arms round Dimanche. They sat together for several minutes without speaking. Then Dimanche put her hand up and carefully investigated whatever it was that had hit her. "It's gnarly," she whispered, "and hard, with moss on. It's an oak tree, I can tell by the bark.

She's rolled a log across the opening."

"We'll never lift it, Dimanche. She must have used a lever."

"Have you got any matches, Polly?"

Polly generally had some for lighting fires, but now she shook her head. "I left them with the camping things in Papa Fettler's caravan. We couldn't burn the log anyway, Dimanche, we'd choke to death on the smoke before we got out."

Dimanche's head hurt badly where she'd hit it against the log. She put a finger to the spot and it came away sticky. She was bleeding – not much, but not much is too much when it comes to blood. Her hand and knees stung sharply from where she'd landed on them when she fell, and she was dying for the loo. Worst of all, she was terrified of the dark. A dark wet cellar is not a pleasant place to be if you're afraid of the dark, even if you can walk back out when you want to. To be trapped in one is dreadful.

Polly knew all about Dimanche being scared of the dark. Long ago she had bought, out of her own wages, a little pink night light, and put it on Dimanche's bedside table. It was left on all night in spite of everything Valburga said about wasting electricity and pulling yourself together. Sensing Dimanche's panic, Polly recalled an old spell she'd made up when Dimanche was younger, and hated bedtime. She began to recite it now, in the dark cellar.

Shine all night, bedside light,
Flicker white, torch bright.
Candle glow, sweet and low.
Cosy bright, fire light.
Pale and fine, moon shine.
Freckle my skin, sun shine in.
House light, mouse light,
Gnat light, bat light,
Bright light, all night,
SHINE ON ME AND DIMANCHE.

Dimanche got to her feet when Polly had finished and walked slowly down the steps to the bottom. She held her hands out in front of her in case she should meet something else waiting for her to bump into it. She didn't. There was just dark space, and then a damp earth-and-brick wall. Polly joined her, and together they felt all round the walls of the cellar. There was no way out.

A couple of hours later – at about one o'clock in

the morning – Polly and Dimanche wound up their watches and said goodnight to one another. There didn't seem to be anything they could do except wait for daylight, so they intended to try to pass the time by sleeping. They ran through a hopeful kind of checklist first, to try to give themselves confidence.

"Jack will have got to Papa Fettler easily by now," Dimanche began.

"And Papa Fettler will be on his way to help us," Polly agreed.

"Cosmo will have found my letter in the cold frame. He might have come to look for us."

"He will, I bet. He'll know which way we went because I told him where my great aunt lives. But the Chief Superintendent didn't get my letter. So he won't be on his way."

"You tried, though, Polly. It was clever of you to think of writing to him in the first place."

"Not clever enough."

"Verity Victorine will get my letter tomorrow. Or the next day at the latest."

"And then there's Tom Shovel. He'll be keeping an eye on Valburga Vilemile. I wouldn't put it past him to follow her back here."

"All we've got to do, Polly, is keep each other safe until the morning."

They kissed one another goodnight, as they had done every night since Polly came to Hilton Hall, cuddled up close together and shut their eyes. It wasn't any darker with them shut.

At first they could not sleep for more than minutes at a time. The cold of the cellar, and the wet hard steps they were trying to lean on, woke them constantly. Both of them needed the loo and neither of them wanted to be the first to go. Eventually Polly solved it.

"Right, Dimanche," she said. "Over there's the loo. That corner. We'll go together, like we did when you were little."

After that they slept a little better, and around four in the morning they both managed to fall properly asleep and didn't wake again till light was filtering down into the cellar.

Sixteen

Dimanche woke first, as she always did, even in her own comfortable bed. She couldn't move without waking Polly because they were leaning on one another. Polly's face looked white and smudged and tired, so Dimanche sat still, watching and waiting. Little beams shone round the edges of the log that blocked the entrance, just enough to let Dimanche see wet brick walls, and a wet floor with a few patches of moss growing on it and one or two ferns growing out of it. The air was cold and clammy.

Even if the sun shone outside it, it made no difference to the climate in the cellar.

Something moved in the opposite corner – something close to the ground, and about the same colour. Spider? Snake? Whatever it was, it knew she'd spotted it. It kept quite still. Dimanche stared at the place until she found a shape against the shadows: a biggish toad, pale coloured, *probably from spending all its time in a cellar*, she thought. *We'll go pale too if we stay here. Pale as bones. We'll be bones.* It was unpleasant to think about the toad being there all night, close by, and them not seeing it.

Luckily Polly woke up before Dimanche could start thinking really gruesome thoughts. Both of them were hungry, but they hadn't got so much as a biscuit or a packet of crisps between them. Polly began to talk to keep their minds off breakfast.

"That one's a common toad. Natterjacks are smaller. This one's a female – they're bigger than the males. People used to think toads were magic."

"This one could give us three wishes if it was. What's it doing down here? If I was magic I wouldn't stay in a slimy cellar."

"Toads like this sort of place. It probably came down here to hibernate. At this time of year it'll want to be off to find a mate."

"It can't get out."

"Not until we do, no."

"D'you think it'll find a mate, Polly?"

"Sure to. And lay 7000 eggs in a nice cool pond. Then it'll climb out and go and do whatever toads do in the summer. Eat, mainly."

"Why did you say that word, Polly?"

"Sorry."

"What do they eat, Polly?"

"Worms and snails and ants and beetles and caterpillars and woodlice. Anything small that moves, but nothing that doesn't. Sort of opposite to us." Polly and Dimanche didn't eat meat, so the biggest single thing they might tuck into would be something like a vegetable marrow.

"What would you wish for, Dimanche, if you had three wishes?"

They played that game for quite some time. Both of them started by wishing to get out of the cellar. After that Dimanche wished that Valburga Vilemile would fall into a pond and be eaten slowly by giant toads. Polly wished for twelve holidays with Dimanche, each lasting a month, one after the other. By the time they'd chosen where to go and what to do for each month, the cellar was as light as it was going to get, so they began to examine every inch of the walls and roof in case they had missed, in last night's darkness, any weak points or possible escaping places. They hadn't.

Next they spent an hour or more struggling with the tree trunk that blocked off the entrance, but it became clear to them long before they were ready to give up that they couldn't shift it.

"OK," Polly said. "We can't get out. So we must wait for someone else to get in. If it's Valburga Vilemile, I'll try to get her gun. You run for help. If it's anybody else, they'll be on our side. What we've got to do now is make the time pass. Let's try some poetry. We'll start with *Horatius.*"

Dimanche did not falter until she reached verse twenty-one:

> *"And nearer fast and nearer*
> *Doth the red whirlwind come;*
> *And louder still and still more loud,*
> *From underneath that rolling cloud*
> *Is heard…"*

"… the trumpet's war-note proud."
Polly continued for her,
"The trampling, and the hum."

By the time they got to verse seventy, which is the last, they both felt full of optimism. After that they recited *Lochinvar* in their best Scottish accents, followed by *O, my love is like a red, red rose*, by Robert Burns, because *Lochinvar* had made them feel romantic. After that they asked each other riddles. Then they played consequences, then twenty questions, then letters of the alphabet with animals, and then with names and then with fruit. Which meant that they were talking about food again.

"Apple."

"Banana."

"Cantaloupe melon."

"Damson."

"Eggplant."

"Fresh crumpets."

"Fresh crumpets aren't fruit, Dimanche."

"No, but I'd like some."

"Don't," Polly begged. "It only makes it worse. Let's dig a tunnel."

They dug with their hands, and bits of stick they found and poked between bricks to lever them up. They knew it was probably pointless. And there were still great boring acres of the day when they were tired of digging, and had played every word game they could think of two or three times, and still they couldn't stop thinking about food. They licked drops of water off the ferns to try to quench their thirst, which tasted nice, but there was so little of it that it hardly helped at all. Dimanche woke the toad up, but really a toad's no fun to play with, and you certainly can't eat one.

They dozed and chatted, and the time must have passed, but so slowly that they couldn't tell that it was. Every now and then they imagined they heard footsteps. They shouted and banged on the bottom of the tree trunk with their shoes, but either nobody was there, or else the earth muffled their voices. It was a long and dreary day.

Seventeen

Not until the cellar had grown dark at the start of their second night in it did they really hear footsteps, right over their heads. Somebody sat down heavily on the tree trunk.

"Are you enjoying yourselves down there?" called a familiar voice.

"Valburga Vilemile!" Polly shouted. "Let us out of here immediately!"

"Not likely, Miss Pugh. I only came back to make sure you were still down there."

"If we die, Valburga, you'll be guilty of murder."

"But extremely rich," Valburga agreed.

That wicked woman actually sat down to enjoy a picnic, leaving her hungry prisoners below. She ate a lobster salad with an avocado dip, and drank a whole bottle of rather fruity wine. Polly and Dimanche could hear her guzzling from their seat on the cellar steps. As they listened, they became aware of a change in the night sky, although they could not see it. Narrow shafts of moonlight had been shining round the edges of the tree trunk, glinting on the wet floor. But now the cellar was growing darker by the minute.

"There's a storm coming," Dimanche called. "It's going to pour with rain! You'll get absolutely soaked and serve you right! I hope your arthritis gives you hell."

"Rubbish! There's not a cloud in the sky! Your eyesight must be failing," Valburga called. But she did not sound convinced.

The cellar grew darker and darker until the light was entirely gone. Up above, Valburga stood up uncertainly and looked about. The wood was now as dark as the inside of a coffin. And yet there wasn't a cloud in the sky. Stars winked in all the places that they had before, but something was happening to the moon. A minute ago it had been as full as a carp's belly. Now something rather like a giant bowler hat was crawling across its white face. Valburga watched in horror.

If Dimanche or Polly could have seen it they'd have known an eclipse of the moon was under way, but Valburga hadn't got a clue. She thought someone had put a spell on the moon. She thought earthquakes, floods, fires and catastrophes were about to strike her flat. Abandoning her picnic, she began to gather up her long skirts. She was about to run for home when a shimmering soft brown shape crashed through the undergrowth and slid to a stop inches away from her black button boots. The black hat slid slowly off the moon. Light filtered back into the world and turned the shape into a roan pony. Papa Fettler slid off Rosie's back.

"Ill met by moonlight, proud Valburga," he said. "So this is where you're holding my young friends prisoner! Followed 'em through the wood, did you, and took 'em prisoner, and shoved 'em down under ground? Why would you do such a cruel thing? Was it that greed of yours?"

Down in the cellar, Dimanche and Polly shouted with joy. A mean little snick of a click reminded them Valburga had a pistol. Before they could shout a warning to Papa Fettler, two thumps, one on top of the other, rocked the ceiling of their prison, and a strangled squawk told them Valburga was down. Next came Tom Shovel's voice. "Don't hardly seem right, do it, Long Tom?" he said. "Knocking a nun down? It's not a thing I've done before. I don't believe I've ever knocked anybody down, not since I was a lad. What shall I do with her?"

"Sit on her, Tom Shovel, while I get our friends out from under that log."

Eighteen

As Papa Fettler levered the heavy oak log off the entrance
to the cellar, Dimanche felt the night air flow down into
her prison in a crystal stream. She took Polly's hand.
Together they walked up the steps into a spring night
bright with moonlight.

Rosie stood close by, munching a tuft of grass. Jack sat
on top of the oak log, one ear pricked towards Valburga
Vilemile, who lay on the ground under Tom Shovel. Papa
Fettler put one arm round Polly and the other round

Dimanche and the three of them danced a few steps together in the bright clearing. Cosmo, hurrying up from the direction of Hilton Hall, stopped in his tracks and gave them a round of applause. He had a basket in one hand, and Dimanche's letter in the other.

"Is that food you've got in there, Cosmo?" Dimanche asked.

"It is, my poppet. I thought you might fancy a bite of something. I've brought you a Thermos of home-made soup and plenty of fresh bread and butter to be going on with. And a few cakes and some jelly. And some of your favourite cheese, the sort with holes in. And if you're still hungry after that, there's her ladyship's picnic."

The five friends sat in a row on the log and ate. Of course Dimanche and Polly ate far more than anybody else. They gave the crusts to Jack and Rosie and offered some of her own picnic to Valburga Vilemile – who would not have given them a crumb if she had been the winner.

"Victory makes good people magnanimous and bad ones mean," Papa Fettler remarked. "You're one of the bad ones, Valburga Vilemile. It's lucky for you we're not, or we might push you down those cellar steps and roll that log across and leave you there to wane, as you would have left young Dimanche and her Polly. But we're not, so we won't."

Dimanche sighed. She'd felt quite tempted.

"I'll take charge of you for now," Papa Fettler continued. "I'll take you to the police and they can hand you over to the law courts and the judge can decide what happens to you after that."

Valburga did not reply. A tear trickled from the corner of her eye, but it made Dimanche think of crocodiles, not sorrow.

"The rest of you had best get back to Hilton Hall. I believe there's a visitor heading your way, Tom Shovel."

Papa Fettler got to his feet. He and Tom Shovel tied Valburga up with a piece of rope Cosmo had in his basket. They helped her up on to old Rosie's back. Papa Fettler took her bridle and they moved off through the woods.

Cosmo offered Dimanche a piggy-back, which she accepted gratefully. "What about you, Polly? Can you walk?" Cosmo asked. Polly nodded. Dimanche looked sleepily from Cosmo's back to Polly's face. She thought she saw the trace of a blush on Polly's cheeks.

She glanced back once towards the dark hole in the pile of rubble. Something was crawling out of it.

It was the toad, heading for pastures new. Its warty body, crawling laboriously up the steps and on to the grass, was the last thing Dimanche saw before her eyes closed in sleep.

Nineteen

The victory party was held at Hilton Hall three evenings later, when Dimanche and Polly had recovered fully from their imprisonment, Valburga Vilemile had been placed in custody awaiting trial, and the real Verity Victorine had come home to her niece.

Tom Shovel brought her up to the big house. She had gone to his cabin first, as Dimanche had suggested in her letter. She and Tom Shovel talked for a long while before coming up to the Hall. Verity knew all about the hardships Dimanche had suffered at Valburga's hands. She knew about the sinking of the yacht *Hippolytus* and the loss of her sister and brother-in-law. She knew about the Sisters of Small Mercies, and about the love and care Polly Pugh had given Dimanche since she was three years old. She knew about Cosmo's kindness to a lonely child, and Papa Fettler's part in the escape.

When Dimanche met her real Aunt Verity for the first time she found herself looking into a face that was familiar twice over. Verity's curly hair was hidden by her still white coif, but her dark eyebrows and her rich brown eyes, even the freckles on her nose and cheeks, echoed Dimanche's own, and both faces echoed the little photo of Dolores that stood on Dimanche's bedside table next to her night light.

Verity shook Dimanche formally by the hand; both of them felt quite shy. Dimanche suggested a walk, and they set off across the lawns so neatly trimmed by Cosmo, down the yew avenue, over the ha-ha and out into the spring-beginning fields.

Watching them go, Polly could not prevent one or two tears escaping from her eyes. Cosmo put a comforting arm round her shoulders. "She's still your Dimanche, Polly, even if her auntie has come home."

Polly nodded, and smiled at Cosmo. "What about a walk of our own?" she suggested.

Several important things were agreed between Verity and Dimanche during the course of their slow ramble over the fields and under the trees. Verity told Dimanche that her Mother Superior was letting her stay on at Hilton Hall until Dimanche was grown up. Dimanche told Verity that Polly Pugh must stay on too, and Verity agreed that this was what should happen. If Polly should decide to marry, she added, she could have the pick of the Hilton Hall cottages in which to start her family. These matters agreed, they talked about the victory party and made lists in their heads of whom to invite. Lastly, they agreed that Cyclops, though not a pleasant cat, should be allowed to stay at Hilton Hall if Valburga Vilemile ended up in prison. By this time they had stopped feeling shy and were walking with their arms round one another.

When everything that needed settling had been settled, they talked of Darcy and Dolores, and of Valery, Verity's much-loved Frenchman. They talked of Britannia and Bertram, Dimanche's grandparents. They talked of old Tom Shovel, and the strangeness of life, and of Papa Fettler, whom Verity remembered from her own childhood days. "We called him Papa Vittler."

"Tom Shovel calls him Long Tom."

"He's a man of many names, and none the worse for that."

"Did he have a pony called Rosie when you knew him?" Dimanche asked.

"No. He had one called Clary then. And a dog called Mop."

They heard hooves clopping on the lane then and, looking across the valley, saw an old caravan, drawn by a plodding pony. A little figure in a big coat sat above the shafts, with a dog beside him. They were too small to make out any features but there was no doubt who they were. Verity and Dimanche stood in the shade of Darcy's damsons, not waving, because the caravan was still too far away. Papa Fettler looked out across the valley. Dimanche thought she saw a flash of his grey eyes, but knew she couldn't have. She smiled to herself. Papa Fettler lifted his hat and waved.

As the caravan drew closer, Dimanche saw that there were three people sitting in the back under the hooped roof. The canvas was rolled back, the day being fine, and soon Dimanche could see that the figures in the back were wearing coifs and veils and cloaks. Something sweet and soft stirred in her memory. Sea shanties.

A hammock swinging between lilac trees. A cake with golden bees that spelt her name.

One minute she was standing beside Verity Victorine, watching the little caravan creep slowly up the lane from Hilton in the Hollow station, the next she was flying across the fields. "Sister Sophia!" she shouted. "Sister Catriona! It's me! It's me! It's me!"

The two Sisters tumbled out of the back of Papa Fettler's caravan without waiting for him to rein in. Down on to the lane they jumped, through a gap in the hedge and out across the green fields, their white habits twinkling and their cloaks flying out behind. In the middle of the meadow they collided with Dimanche and all three rolled over in a tangle of habits and sandals and bare legs.

Mother Superior asked Papa Fettler to stop. She climbed down carefully – her old bones were troubling her these days – and walked stiffly over the grass to where Sisters Sophia and Catriona were dusting themselves off. "Dimanche," she said, in her quiet voice. "How very good it is to see you."

She might have been going to say more, but her voice was drowned in the roar of a powerful motorbike. Chief Superintendent Barry Bullpit, summoned by Old Tom Shovel and wearing his off-duty outfit of black leather and goggles, squealed to a stop just behind Papa Fettler's caravan. A less sensible horse than Rosie might have bolted, but she just looked round, blinked, and went on eating the verge. Beryl Bullpit was sitting in the sidecar of Barry's powerful machine, and on the back Winston, still in his railways uniform, sat smiling. He had overheard Papa Fettler talking to the Sisters of Small Mercies on the station, and all at once, remembering that small baby in her big black pram, had felt he'd like to join the celebrations.

The Victory Party started at teatime and finished the following morning. Polly's Great Aunt Angelica arrived by taxi from the station, in time for Polly and Dimanche to thank her for the help she would have given, had they reached the sanctuary of her house. During the course of the evening, Verity Victorine worked out an excellent plan for the nuns of her Order to visit the Sisters of Small Mercies, and vice versa, making regular holidays abroad a feature of both convents.

Barry Bullpit brought news of Valburga's impending trial, and stated that in his opinion she could get as much as seven years, what with kidnapping, attempted murder, and impersonating a nun. Winston offered to be a witness at her trial and give evidence of her unkindness to baby Dimanche, left alone in the luggage compartment with only a bottle of cold tea.

Papa Fettler played the fiddle, Polly played the harmonica and Cosmo the tin whistle. Everyone danced. Towards midnight Polly said she had an announcement to make. She left the room covered in blushes and without having made it, and had to be brought back by Cosmo, who made it for her. He and Polly were going to be married.

Dimanche felt very happy. Valburga's days were over and gone. Aunt Verity was here to stay. Polly would marry Cosmo and live in the cottage close by Hilton Hall. When they have children, she thought, I will take them for walks and show then all the best places to play.

Moonlight filled the valley. Cyclops lay on the garden wall digesting his dinner. He didn't miss his mistress in the least – unlike her, he was all bad.

Down under Darcy's damsons two shadows stirred. The ghosts of Darcy and Dolores turned to one another, smiling. Dimanche was safe. Confident now of her lasting happiness, their faint grey figures melted into night. Only Tom Shovel and Papa Fettler saw them go.

Papa Fettler raised his fiddle in salute, and Old Tom Shovel bowed. Dimanche looked up at them, puzzled, for a moment, before turning back to the dance.

MORE THAN A STORY

CONTENTS PAGE

FAMOUS ORPHANS

Losing your father and your mother is a terrible thing. But in history, many people have been taken away from their parents at a very young age and have grown up to be amazing, interesting and successful people. Here are a few:

Leo Tolstoy's mother died when he was two and his father a few years later. He wrote *War and Peace*, one of the most famous books ever written.

Nelson Mandela's father died when he was 9 and he was brought up by a local chief. He fought all his life for black people's right to be treated fairly and became the first black president of South Africa.

John Lennon's parents split up when he was three and he went to live with his aunt and uncle. When he was 15 he formed a band which became famous all round the world as **The Beatles.**

Marilyn Monroe never knew her father and her mother was so ill that little Marilyn was sent off to a series of orphanages. But she grew up to be a famous film star and a friend of the president of the USA.

Henry Stanley grew up without either a father or mother but he became one of the most famous explorers ever. Another explorer, David Livingstone, had been lost in Africa for many months, and when Stanley found him, his first words were, 'Doctor Livingstone, I presume?'

Johann Sebastian Bach was a famous musician and the youngest of eight children. He was only 9 when both his parents died but he grew up to write some of the most brilliant and beautiful music in the world.

The philosopher **Aristotle** was an orphan, and so was the Roman Emperor **Caesar Augustus. Wordsworth** the poet was an orphan and so was **Queen Victoria of England.** In fiction, some of the most famous characters are orphans: think of **Harry Potter**, or **James** in Roald Dahl's *James and the Giant Peach*.

AUNTIES AND UNCLES...

My aunty who came from Dundee
Once climbed up a very high tree
She felt quite a clown
When she couldn't get down -
She's been stuck there since 2003.

I once had an uncle called Neil
Who went for a ride on a seal.
He would have survived
If the seal hadn't dived
And the shark hadn't wanted a meal!

Aunty Adds

Aunty: Rosie, if I give you 3
kittens today and 3 kittens
tomorrow, how many will
you have?
Rosie: 7
Aunty: 7?
Rosie: I've got one already, you see!

BRAIN-TEASERS
AND
MIND BENDERS!

Polly taught Dimanche all kinds of important
things, like how to:

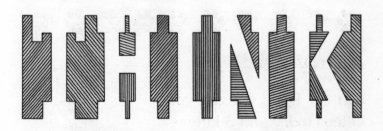

Can you see the word? If you didn't,
look it up in the back.

Here are some puzzles to make you think.
See if you can work them out. Try them out
on your friends.

Moon madness

Look at these two pictures for 3 seconds.
Spot anything wrong?

What can you see?
Check your answer in the back.

A hole lot of trouble

You're playing with a ping-pong ball and it falls
down a hole. You want to get it back, but the
hole is deeper than your arm is long. You haven't
got a long stick. What can you do?

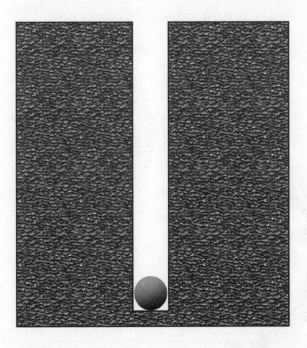

The paper cup problem

Get six paper cups and put a little water in three of them.

How can you change the line-up so that no glass with water is next to another glass with water – and no empty is next to another empty.

You can only move ONE CUP.

POLLY'S RIDDLES

All in the Family

A boy went to the dentist to have a filling. The boy was the dentist's son, but the dentist wasn't the boy's father. How come?

Answer: the dentist was the boy's mother!

What has four legs and cannot walk?

Answer: a chair.

What goes up when the rain comes down?

Answer: an umbrella.

What did the baby porcupine say when he backed into a cactus?

Answer: is that you, Mum?

TRAVELLER'S TART

This is a gorgeous gooey tart which Dimanche loved long before she met Papa Fettler.

You need:

1 packet frozen short crust pastry. (Some people like to make this themselves: see below)*

1 large tin evaporated milk

275g soft dark brown sugar. (Muscovado is best)

*Sweet short crust pastry

What you need:

175 g plain flour

110 g butter

1 teaspoonful sugar

pinch of salt

1 egg yolk

a few drops of water

What you do:

- Mix everything together except the water and egg yolk (if you have a food processor use this, but get a grown up to help you). The mixture should look like bread crumbs.

- Now add the egg yolk and a few drops of water. The mixture will be very stiff. Roll it into a ball.

- Get a grown up to turn on the oven to 200 degrees C, Gas Mark 6.

- Roll out the pastry and line a 23cm flan tin.

- Now line the pastry with tin foil. (This is called 'baking blind' and the tin foil is to stop the pastry bubbling up).

- Get a grown up to put the pastry in the oven for 10 –15 minutes, checking that it isn't burning. It's done when it is a nice, pale brown colour. Take off the foil.

Now for the tart:

- Whisk the evaporated milk and the sugar together until the mixture is thick, light and creamy. Ask an adult to help.

- Pour the mixture onto the cooked pastry and get an adult to put it in the oven for 20-25 minutes.

- The filling will still be a little gooey, but don't panic. Leave it to cool by itself. (Don't put it in the fridge or the topping will split)

- Cut into delicious sweet and creamy slices and eat with cream or ice cream – or just on its own.

FINAL FUN AND GAMES

Secret Letters

Polly thought up a clever code to beat evil aunt Valburga.
Here is Polly's message for Dimanche:

"TEEM EM TA THGINDIM YB EHT KCAB SRIATS"

Clue: think backwards!

If you have a special secret message of your own, why
not put it in code?

Tomato Ketchup

Polly is good at thinking up games. She and
Dimanche spend a lot of time making each other
laugh. Try this game yourself.

The person who is 'it', has to reply 'tomato ketchup'
to every question WITHOUT LAUGHING.

So: someone might ask: 'what do you look like?'
and you would have to answer: 'tomato ketchup.'
The harder you try not to laugh, the more you
want to giggle! Even if you smile you are
out and the person who asked the
question is 'it'.

Hidden holidays

....

Valburga never gave Polly and Dimanche a penny to go on holiday. Can you unscramble these countries to find out where they'd like to go?

CEFRAN, NAISP, RIAFCA, ACHIN, ECEGRE, DIANI

Then Polly saved up to take Dimanche away. Where was it?

My first is in **wishing** but not in **fishing**
My second is in **wave** but not in **wove**
My third is in **lake** but not in **make**
My fourth is in **seat** but not in **sat**
My fifth is in **sun** but not in **run**.

Papa Fettler to the Rescue!

Which road will take Papa Fettler to save Polly and Dimanche without meeting Aunt Valburga or her horrible cat, Cyclops?

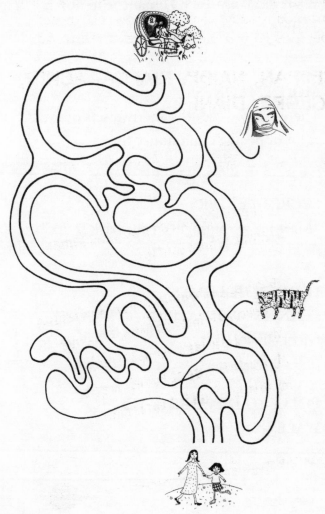

ANSWERS

What did Polly teach Dimanche to do?
THINK

MOON MADNESS
There are two mouths and two sets of eyes.
A lot of people don't notice this.

SECRET LETTERS
"Meet me at midnight by the back stairs."

HIDDEN HOLIDAYS
FRANCE, SPAIN, AFRICA, CHINA,
GREECE, INDIA

POLLY TO DIMANCHE TO:
WALES